IF YOU GIVE A HELLION YOUR HEART

CHLOE FLOWERS

F&F
Flowers and Fullerton

IF YOU GIVE A HELLION YOUR HEART

NOT 'TIL DEATH WILL SHE PART

Pirates & Petticoats Book 3

Remember me...
His memory of her is gone.
Bounty hunters are closing in.
Her fight for his love soon turns into a fight for his life.

❦

*NOTE: This book (formally known as Hart's Reward) is the *sexy version* of the novel *The Heart of a Bride*, (Book 3 of The Hearts of Adventure Sweet Romance Series By Chloe Flowers).

❦

An accident robs Landon Hart of his memory and turns his new wife Keelan into a complete stranger.

Landon is thrown back five years into his past, to a point just after a horrendous betrayal by his late wife. Not only does he refuse to believe Keelan is his new wife, he's convinced that he'd never have married again.

Worse, a series of catastrophic events has Landon accusing Keelan of conspiracy and betrayal. When each explanation sounds more and more outlandish, her hope for Landon to remember her love becomes more and more futile. Bounty hunters are closing in, and a nefarious plantation owner has discovered Landon's secret identity. More than ever, Keelan needs Landon's on her side if she's going to save both their lives.

Can she persuade him to trust her? Will he remember his love for her before it's too late?

If you love romance swirled with adventure and intrigue, you'll love reading about Landon and Keelan's road to their happily ever after, because true love will always find a way.

TWO LOVERS OR TWO STRANGERS?

Landon's eyes widened and traveled from Keelan's face down to her bare breasts, then over her boy's breeches and boots then back up again.

"What in God's name...." He clenched his jaw and in two strides closed the space between them. His movement finally broke her temporary paralysis and she lunged for her shirt still draped over their bed. His bed now, since he had no memory of ever sharing it with her.

He reached her before she could take a second step, grabbed her arm and pushed her against the wall of the cabin. His crystalline irises flashed in anger. "Who the hell are you?" His gaze raked once more past her stained face, neck and chest to her creamy white breasts and pale stomach.

"And no more lies," he growled.

If he expected her to shrink in fear, he was going to be disappointed. Keelan lifted her chin and glared back at him as best as she could, considering the top of her head barely reached his jaw.

No more tiptoeing around the truth, then.

"I am Keelan O'Brien Hart. Your *wife*."

BOOKS BY CHLOE FLOWERS

If you enjoy reading about strong heroines, charming smugglers and sweet romance mixed with action, intrigue and a few laughs you'll love these series!

Want SWEET historical romance instead?

Read The Hearts of Adventure Series (the Sweet version of Pirates & Petticoats)

The Heart of a Tempest

The Heart of a Siren

The Heart of a Bride

The Heart of a Pirate

The Heart of a Spy

Enjoy Sexy Historical Romance?

Pirates & Petticoats is for you!

If You Give a Smuggler a Secret

If You Give a Rake a Reason

If You Give a Hellion Your Heart

If You Give a Pirate a Treasure

If You Give a Spy a Scheme

THE HART TRILOGY

If You Give a Smuggler a Secret, If You Give a Rake a Reason and *If You Give a Hellion Your Heart* is a trilogy that follows Keelan Grey and Landon Hart on their adventure of discovery and a love of a lifetime. Two hearts have never battled more fiercely to be together...

IF YOU GIVE A SMUGGLER A SECRET

He'll Demand a Kiss to Keep It

A lady plotting her way out of an arranged marriage,

A smuggler with a cryptic invitation to a clandestine meeting,

A group of pirates out for revenge.

It's the perfect storm.

IF YOU GIVE A RAKE A REASON

He'll Covet a Caress to Please Him

A deathbed confession.

A dark plot of revenge.

A band of ticked off pirates.

What else could possibly go wrong?

IF YOU GIVE A HELLION YOUR HEART

Then Not 'til Death Will She Part

Remember me...

An accident rips sway the last five years of his life,

And turns his new bride into a stranger.

Her fight for his love soon turns into a fight for his life.

❧

Other Pirates & Petticoats novels:

IF YOU GIVE A PIRATE A TREASURE

She'll Steal your Heart for Good Measure

Her twin siblings have been kidnapped.

The ransom is a ship called The Seeker.

She's not a real pirate.

But their lives depend on her playing the part.

❧

IF YOU GIVE A SPY A SCHEME

He'll Fight to be Redeemed

He steals for the French crown.

She heals for the Catholic church.

He will heal her heart.

She will steal his.

❧

Coming soon: A new sweet contemporary small town romance series sure to capture your heart and tickle your funny bone.

BRIDAL VEIL FALLS

The town of Happily Ever Afters

CHLOE'S WEBSITE: WWW.CHLOEFLOWERS.COM

DISCLAIMER

This book is a work of fiction.
Names, characters, places and incidents are the product of the author's imagination or are used fictitiously. Any resemblance to actual people, (living or dead) events or places is entirely coincidental.

AUTHOR'S NOTE

Not long ago, my son was in an accident and received a hard blow to the head. What followed, for me as a parent, was one of the most terrifying few weeks of my life. The concussion was severe enough to keep him under a specialists care for four long months.

To this day, he has no recollection of the accident or even of that day. As a volleyball coach, I've been trained to recognize signs of concussion. Here are some symptoms:

- Memory fog
- Sluggishness
- Dizziness
- Nausea
- Sensitivity to light and/or noise
- Headache and/ or blurred vision

Here are questions you can ask to check for memory problems:

- What's the date?
- What did you have for breakfast?

- State the last 5 letters of the alphabet backwards, starting with "Z"
- Give them a random 4 digit number and ask them to recite it to you backwards.

If they struggle with any of these questions, or show any of the symptoms, seek medical attention right away.

DEDICATION

This book is dedicated to my parents, husband and children,
who have supported me and encouraged me in realizing my dream of
becoming a writer.
To Bonnie LaBadie, you know why.
Kathy Wilhelm, you rock.

A huge thanks to NorthEast Ohio Romance Writers and Romance Writers
of America for providing the resources, the mentorship and especially the
friendships. I'm a better writer because of you ladies!
To the Sunshine Critique Group: Kate Pembrooke, Wendy Larkin,
Miranda Liasson
Victoria Sheridan, and Sheridan Jeane.
You chix are the best!
Love and smooches to you all.

***D*ON'T *FORGET TO TRY OUR SECRET FAMILY RECIPE AT THE END OF THE BOOK FOR *F*RIED *P*IES!**

Chloe

CHAPTER 1

July 1811
Harbour Town, Georgia

Keelan rolled over and nuzzled Landon's neck. His chest vibrated with a satisfied hum. She kissed the place where his pulse surfaced, then stroked small circles around his heart. It beat strongly beneath her fingers.

"Good morning, love," he murmured. "Did you sleep well?"

Keelan smiled and kissed his shoulder. "I slept well, but not long. Although I'm not complaining."

Landon ran a gentle hand down her side to her hip and pulled her closer before caressing the naked curve of her bottom. "Should I apologize?"

Her breath hitched. "Absolutely not." She snuggled closer and kissed his chest. "I'm enjoying my role as a new bride."

Landon's hand stilled. "Keelan, I'm sorry we couldn't be properly wed in Harbour Town. If things had gone as I'd planned—"

"It isn't your fault." She placed her hand over his and brought it to her heart. "No one could have predicted yesterday's events." Things had certainly *not* gone as planned.

His chest rose and fell with a deep sigh. "Making you my wife in the eyes of the church is important. To both of us."

Keelan squeezed Landon's hand. "We shall wed when the time is right."

"I promised." Landon's expression gave her pause. Here was a man unused to his commands falling unheeded. He gave his men an order, and they completed it. Nothing more to say about it, no argument, no discussion, no debate.

"Landon Hart, you listen to me." She placed her other hand on his cheek and captured his gaze. "The promise you gave to me in front of God, my protector Daniel, and my brother when we hand-fasted is enough. I love you with all my heart. I trust you with all my heart. I don't need a dry piece of parchment to tell me what I already know. We belong to each other."

Landon brought their interlaced fingers to his lips and kissed them. "I love you, Keelan. I *promise*, as soon as we deliver the cargo to Philadelphia, I'll seek out a priest to marry us. Then we shall set sail to rescue your brother."

"I believe you." She smiled. As badly as she wanted to chase after her brother's kidnappers, there were other lives depending on Landon Hart. His dedication to the Freedom Runners proved he was indeed a man of honor, even if he was a smuggler (she'd decided to avoid thinking about *that* little side-business of his). Trusting him had been hard. It had meant she'd had to take her pride and stow it—far away from the warning seeds her foster mother had been so careful to plant about the lascivious lives of men of the sea.

"I know it took me a long time to trust you," Keelan murmured. The woman who'd raised her had been a bitter shell of a wife left alone while her husband sailed for the Royal Navy. When Keelan learned that Catherine Grey wasn't her actual mother, she'd been relieved, actually. Catherine had shown no affection for Keelan, and spent most of her time in her shop in Chatham, England, leaving Keelan to be raised by a maid and the valet, Daniel. "Then I came to know you, and the man you are. How could I not fall in love with you?" She pressed her hand over Landon's heart. "You asked me to join you, and I have."

Landon rubbed his thumb over the top of her hand. "Still, I gave you my word, and I'll see we are legally wed as soon as possible." He gave her a pained grin. "Your brother Conal may be content with our hand fast, but I know your mother, and she'll have a word or two to say if I escort you across her threshold before a priest deems us married."

She tapped the scar on his chin with her finger. "Then we must do everything we can to keep you in her good graces." Kidnapped from her crib as a toddler, Keelan had not yet met her parents. It was all the more reason to finish their business and find her brother, so Conal could take her home to meet her real family.

Landon took a pensive breath. "We need to make a quick docking in Charleston to pick up the last group of runaways and then we'll set sail northward." Concern seeped into his eyes. Worry that the price on her head in Charleston would muddy up the sediment that had settled into the dark places there. "Lower men who hold no honor or pride will seek you out for Gampo's reward." True, the pirate Gampo had departed the city, but he'd left a message at the docks regarding Keelan Grey.

She gave him a smile, showing a confidence she didn't quite feel. "Mrs. Schoen has seen that I'm well-disguised. They'll never know I've returned." The tavern keeper's wife at The Whistling Pig had helped her dye her skin and hair. Keelan had passed as a Persian galley boy on her brother's ship easily enough. "We can pick up the runaways and sail north before anyone is the wiser."

Two entities, The Freedom Runners and Ahern Shipping, had formed an easy partnership. It was well known that single runaways had a greater chance of success, but families, with children, less so. Landon focused on freeing families, even though the danger was greater. Keelan's thoughts shifted to Gampo and a chilled shiver trickled up her spine. "Perhaps my name will have been forgotten. Do you think I'll still be in danger in Charleston?" It was a half-hearted optimism that made her ask, even though the answer was likely one she'd rather not hear.

Keelan thought of Gampo, and a chilled shiver trickled up her spine. "Perhaps my name will have been forgotten. Do you think I'll still be in danger in Charleston?" It was a half-hearted optimism that made her ask, even though the answer was obvious.

Landon's jaw clenched as it rested against her head and she took that to mean 'yes.' "Gampo left word on the docks he wanted you alive. Although a rumor has surfaced that all that's needed to collect the reward, is a token from your head," he said.

The skin on her scalp tingled.

If only she didn't have such a distinguishable head of hair. Once, the curls had been long enough to brush her waist. God had also graced her with a deep auburn color; a cross between a chestnut brown and burnished copper, hence Gampo's conciliatory acceptance of a piece her scalp.

Landon reached up and smoothed her curls. "You must remain *Mahdi*, our Persian galley boy, until we depart Charleston," he said. He was concerned, but she could still hear the smile in his voice. Perhaps he was thinking back to the day he discovered her disguised as Mahdi. That morning, she'd fallen into the brass bathing tub while he occupied it. Her disguise had been brilliant until he noticed the line of demarcation across her chest where the applied stain met the pale white of her natural skin.

"When will we reach Charleston?" It was imperative that they complete this mission quickly. The next one, chasing after her brother, would be no less dangerous.

"Less than a day. The quicker we can pick up our cargo there, the sooner we can head for Philadelphia."

Other Freedom Runners would take the runaways from port

and send them on their way to Canada. Then she and Landon would sail for Jamaica to catch up with her cousin Brendan and rescue her brother Conal. She tried not to think of an alternative ending to that story.

Landon's tone was strong and confident. "With both the *Desire* and the *Reward* on their tail, the pirates who stole your brother's ship will not find a place to hide in Jamaica," he promised.

She couldn't help but ask. "Do you know what started the animosity between Gampo and Fynn?"

Landon took a deep breath and exhaled. "No, but we're determined to end it. It's my hope there are no more lives lost because of it." He brushed the ringlets from her face. "Fynn was the first casualty. For twenty years those two acted more like a couple of toothless dogs than ruthless enemies."

Keelan discovered she had a family and siblings just a day ago. Losing that connection so soon after finding it would be unbearable. "Can we negotiate a truce?"

"Perhaps," he kissed her forehead, "if we get there in time. Your brother sometimes needs a voice of reason. He tends to act first and ask questions second."

"Are you saying that he's impetuous?" She poked him in the ribs.

White teeth flashed in a grin that nearly stilled her heart. "It must be a family trait."

Landon's finger followed the curve of her shoulder. "While you have learned to act the part of a fourteen-year-old boy with a fair amount of success, I fear your brother would fail, in a most miserable fashion, disguised as a girl."

Thinking of her older brother's neatly trimmed beard and upper arms as thick as her thighs, she had to agree.

With that, Landon pulled her on top of him and gave her a long, languid kiss. His mouth moved more urgently against hers, and she thrilled in the heady passion they shared for each other.

Her heartbeat quickened, and she trailed her lips over his neck, kissing the tender spot beneath his ear. His skin was a golden brown from the sun, his chest covered with a light brush of dark hair and hard, chiseled muscle.

He stroked her hair. "You've stolen my heart, love, and burrowed so deeply into my soul you've become a part of it."

"There's no other place I'd rather be," she murmured. "I love you."

"And I love you."

She kissed him and he stirred against her. Azure eyes smoldered with passion and his mouth quirked up into a slow seductive grin. They were going to be late. Again.

※

IT WAS SOMETIME LATER BEFORE they emerged to the main deck. Keelan finished tying her hair back in a long scarf, while she trailed behind Landon, once again playing the part of a galley boy. Gus, Landon's first mate, stood at the helm, gazing out over the ocean. Landon followed the old salt's gaze and clenched his jaw.

"Well, that don't look good," Gus said, jutting his shaggy chin toward the west.

Keelan caught her breath. Swift, low moving gray clouds formed an enormous anvil shaped wall that consumed half the horizon. In the distance, lighter gray sheets of rain fell beneath it.

Gus swallowed. "That ain't no pitter-patter, spring shower."

"We'll not have the speed to skirt it," Landon said. "Shorten the sail. Bring in the top gallants, main and mizzen top sails, and out the small jib."

"Aye, sir." Gus responded, before relaying his captain's orders.

Sailors scampered up the ratlines. They'd also put the runaway slaves to tasks, and a few followed the sailors to the tops. She held her breath as the men soon became the size of swallows perched up in the yards.

Keelan tried to help the crew prepare for the storm. She grabbed a rope when told, pulled when told, let the rope slack when told. Thankfully, the men were aware she was green, so they took extra care to detail their instructions. Soon, many of the big sails were reefed and secured snugly to the yard arms.

The broad shouldered first mate lumbered up next to her.

"Gus, why are we hauling in the sails?" It seemed more logical to take advantage of the increased wind speed and sail as fast as they could away from the storm.

"Yer see, boy, that kinda blow would catch them big sheets and send the stern flying off leeward," Gus said. "Good way to capsize yer ship. We're gonna heave to and wait the storm out." He raised his grizzled face to the wind. "Good thing, too. Blow's picking up."

As if to prove his point, a portion of the shoulder-length hair Keelan had pulled back slipped free from beneath her hat. She tucked it behind her ear. Dark and foreboding, the clouds crowded the ocean. Thousands of white caps dotted the water as the wind churned the sea. Even now, the *Desire* rolled between the growing swells.

How dangerous was it, this gale?

Keelan tied the chin strap to keep her hat from flying away. How easy would it be for a huge swell to cap over and fall on the *Desire*, filling her with ocean water?

Landon had once told her he'd sailed through and around many storms. That should help her feel more confident.

Should.

Still, it was hard to quell the unease. She'd seen the destruction hurricanes left in their wake. Twisted trees, flooded fields, tattered homes.

Daniel, loyal valet to the man who'd raised her, was also on deck, lending a hand to the ropes and securing large barrels around the main mast. He'd stained his skin like hers in order to disguise himself as her father. She ran over to help.

Daniel had been part of Keelan's life for as long as she could remember. He'd taught her not only how to read and do sums but also to fence and duel with swords. With the commodore out at sea for months at a time, and Caroline tending a shop in town, Daniel said it was important for her to learn ways to protect herself. It had been an enjoyable distraction. Those skills had already come in handy more than once.

"What can I do?" Staying busy might keep her mind off the storm.

"Tie this off," Daniel grunted between pulls, "while I keep the line tight."

Keelan had seen the different knots sailors used to secure lines to belaying pins or clews, but wasn't quite sure which knot was proper in this situation, so she tied it the best she could, and wrapped the end of the rope around the knot several times and tucked it in.

"Mahdi!"

It took her half a beat before she found the source of the shout. Forgetting to acknowledge her alias would raise suspicion. It was important that she play the part of Mahdi everywhere but in Landon's cabin. The galley cook already seemed a bit unsure of her. The less attention she attracted, the better.

Landon hailed her from the helm. "Go below!" He shouted into the rising wind. "Help Mister Marcel secure the galley and the cargo."

She nodded and headed toward a small hatch located closest to the kitchen, but couldn't resist a glance over her shoulder at the monster on the horizon. The clouds were churning and flashing in the distance, nearly colliding with the sea.

A dark feeling of foreboding crept up her spine.

CHAPTER 2

A long, lithe, orange cat darted past Keelan as she walked down the narrow passageway to the galley. She poked her head around the corner. Marcel wrestled a barrel toward a closet along with Yanda, a young brown-skinned girl. Now that they were safely away from port, the family of runaways had come out of hiding to help the crew.

"Mahdi! Where have you been, boy?" Marcel drove his hip in to the barrel, but it only moved an inch. "Come, help us."

"Captain Hart had me helping with the ropes. What can I do here?"

The little girl clutched her stomach. Marcel harrumphed and glared at her while he rocked the barrel forward in small steps, "Dozens of men to help with ze sails and no one helps old Marcel."

"Where is Elle?" Keelan asked Marcel. Yanda's mother, Elle, had been a cook for her last master, so it seemed practical to place her in the galley.

"She iz checking the cabinets in zee next room, making sure they are latched." He glanced up at Keelan and muttered, "Useless lubbers, both of zem."

When Elle stumbled in from the next cabin, arms pressed against her belly, Keelan understood and took pity. The woman glistened with sweat. Her eyes were red and her face ashen.

Seasickness. It's hard to want to do anything but die when hit with that kind of nausea.

Marcel gestured to the other side of the barrel. "It iz heavy, but we must lock it in zere. You push, I pull, eh?"

She nodded and together they wiggled the cask into the narrow pantry closet while Marcel spat a string of French curses at the stubbornness of the barrel, at Elle's lack of strength and Yanda, who paused to vomit on the floor. After they secured it, he pointed to a bucket of sea water and a mop and the girl nodded with a mumbled, "Sorry, Monsieur."

They secured the pantry shelves to prevent items from pitching to the floor in rough seas. Marcel placed a tin of dried meat, biscuits and a couple rounds of cheese handy before he shut the door. He nonchalantly pressed a broken biscuit into Yanda's palm on his way out and popped the other half into his mouth.

From there they moved elsewhere on the orlop deck, tying down loose items or stowing them. Port holes were closed and locked, although seawater had already surged in. They trudged through an inch of water on the lower decks. The ship pitched and groaned. Keelan caught her breath and listened to the *Desire's* inhalations and exhalations. Would it stay together through the storm or break into pieces? She studied the beams. Like huge fingers clutching a vase, they held the squirming ship in their grasp. The vessel squealed and moaned her pain and distress.

Marcel, sensing Keelan's trepidation, pointed to the water which had seeped in. "Iz from the hause bucklers."

At her confused expression, he tried again. "Zee pressing of zee ship against the water when swells come, push water through zee house bucklers. The *Desire*, she iz strong and brave. And nimble as a cat. No reason to worry. We sailed through worse."

As they finished, a large group of weary crewmen came below and collapsed at the tables propped between the guns on the gun deck. Marcel jerked his head toward the galley and they went to prepare the meal, which would be nothing more than a piece or two of dried beef, hard biscuits, grog and a chunk of cheese.

The lurch and groans of the ship had Keelan gripping edges of the tables as she staggered past. She'd been getting used to being on the water, and actually enjoyed it, before today. She still moved like a landlubber however, and was anxious to develop her "sea legs." Lanterns swung in unison, casting quick shadows followed by fans of light. The *Desire* pitched sharply and Keelan stumbled. A burly arm shot out and grabbed her collar.

"Careful, boy," Gus said. "Best ye find a spot and stay there."

"How do you keep your footing when the ship bucks and tilts?" She was breathless from her effort to stay upright.

Gus sat back and scratched his salt and pepper beard then gripped his tankard before it flew to the floor. "Seein' how yer father is a horsemaster, I'll put it this way..." He finished his grog. "When the horse jumps a hedge, do ye try and keep yer seat straight and still on the saddle?"

At last. Here was something with which Keelan was familiar, although she hadn't jumped a horse since she was twelve. She shook her head. "You'd fall off if you tried to keep your seat on the saddle. You must stand in the stirrups and keep your legs soft to absorb the impact of the landing."

Gus cocked his head. "Ye Persians sure use peculiar language, but aye. So, ye does the same thing on the water. Mount the *Desire* as ye would a proud filly. Ye'll never tame her, so don't try. All ye can do is melt into her rhythm. Keep yer knees soft and let her rise up to ye. When she sighs and falls away, don't fight her and try to follow. Let her go. She'll come back to ye in her own time. Keep yer guts even with the horizon and ye won't gets seasick."

Keelan let go of the table and heeded his advice. Sure enough, it was similar to jumping her pony. She'd have to mention this method to poor Elle and Yanda. She grinned her thanks to Gus, then asked, "Where's the captain?"

"He has first watch," Gus replied, dipping his tankard into a bucket hanging from a rope secured to the ceiling. "Best fer ye to stay below, outta the way, though."

After serving the men their rations for the evening, she helped Marcel secure the galley before she went back to the cabin. The room tilted and shifted, causing her feet to slide and her stomach to slam into her ribs.

Keep my guts even with the horizon. Keep my guts even with the horizon.

Relaxing her legs, she allowed the *Desire* to take the lead in this rolling dance. A powerful wave hit the ship, and she was surprised and happy with the way she rode it. Now that Gus had revealed the secret to handling the motion, it was much easier to move about. Although it would probably be even easier if she could see the horizon.

She slipped a couple biscuits in her pocket for Landon and left the galley to make her way to the ladder and up to the main deck. Was he alone at the helm? She'd forgotten to ask Gus. If so, perhaps he might like some company.

When she raised the hatch, a lash of stinging sea spray hit her full in the face. The main deck forward sloshed with water, and the entire ship rose and fell in a furious coupling with the sea. The waves crashed against the ship's sides and exploded into the air, spraying the decks.

For a second, she hesitated. Her old self might retreat below to stay dry, but the boy, Mahdi, would be more courageous, wouldn't he? She looked toward the helm. Her husband's form was barely visible through the torrent. If Landon could brave the gale, so could she. Had she not once raced a horse through similar weather, trying to beat a terrible storm? This couldn't be any worse than that.

Keelan climbed out and took a step. The deck jolted, as if trying to fling her away from the safety of the hold. Everything was shiny and slick with seawater. Her feet flew away from her and the tilt of the ship sent her crashing to the boards. Gasping, wet and bruised, she pulled herself to her feet by grasping the lines attached to a belaying pin.

Terror pulsed through her limbs. This was a mistake. She shouldn't have come up on deck. She'd underestimated the power of the ship and the winds and the storm. Landon was only a hundred yards away, but he might as well have been in China. Through sheer will and self-preservation, she struggled to gain her footing in time for the *Desire* to send her tumbling toward midships, her shriek of alarm flung into the sea by the wind.

Panic ripped through her chest. Unless she found some sort of solid purchase, she'd soon be flung like a piece of cloth into the furious ocean. Rolling across the glistening boards that locked together to form the bones, the sinew, and the skin of the *Desire,* she splayed her hands and legs hoping to catch something, *anything*, as the brave vessel heaved against the rage of the ocean.

She tumbled against the side of the ship. Thank goodness there was a plethora of ropes secured to belaying pins, providing something to grasp while she struggled to her feet. The ship fell into another swell and just as she gained her footing, her feet flew away from her again, and she hit the deck hard, her breath knocked from her chest. Before she had time to inhale, the *Desire* saw fit to pour her into a space between two of the petite guns on the deck, instead of tossing her into the sea. She curled her cold, wet fingers around the thick ropes securing the gun and held on for all she was worth.

If she'd had the time, she might have screamed or sobbed in fear, but the tempest didn't permit a pause for such frivolous displays. It only continued to pound the ocean like a giant child throwing a tantrum, plunging the left fist into the water, then the right...

Keelan peered through the rain back to the hatch leading into the hold, then the distance to the helm, and then to Landon. Retracing her steps back below was more treacherous than continuing her fight to the helm at this point. It took every ounce of strength and courage to release her grip from the ropes and drive forward, where two other sailors were clinging on to the wheel with Landon, straining to keep the ship from broaching into the sea.

The thrumming, creaking and whistling of the ropes, lines and spars cracked and whined in her ears. The wind and rain pelted her skin. She'd no idea the storm had become so viscous while she'd been below. In her defense, she'd no idea what to expect of it, but then again, she'd never been one to take heed of a storm warning, had she?

To say that the journey toward the helm was arduous would have been grossly understating the event. If she'd been any less stubborn, she'd never have made it. The bowsprit reared up skyward as if to impale the turbulent clouds, making Keelan's legs as heavy as stone. Then it swooped down to crash into the waves in a violent explosion of white, which had her teetering on her toes, light as a mouse. She finally made it past the main mast encircled with the barrels she and Daniel had secured earlier. Only a few paces to go, thank God.

Several smaller sails were still in service, their sheets flat and rigid in the wind. Shielding her eyes against the salt spray, she sought Landon. His feet were braced wide, and he was heaving his broad chest into the wheel. His dark wet curls whipped around his face, his jaw set. She pulled herself toward the companion ladder that led up to where he stood. Almost there.

"Keelan!"

His shout stopped her. There was a note of panic in his voice that made her pause. He waved his arm. "Move leeward! Starboard!"

Confused, she froze.

"To your right!"

A loud crack followed by a low rumble sounded behind her and she turned as the barrels around the main mast came loose. They rolled away, toward the front of the ship. One hit the foremast and split open, spilling sand across the deck. The bowsprit once again crashed down into the waves.

A jolt of horror shook her limbs. Next, the front of the ship would rear back up and when it did, the barrels would reverse direction and roll toward the stern.

Toward her.

Dear God, help me.

She turned and ran. The pitch of the ship had her running up a steep, slippery slope. A half dozen strides away from her goal, the plume of water hit and shook the front part of the ship. For a second the rumble ceased.

But only for a second.

Panic nearly paralyzed her limbs. The barrels began to roll and bounce toward her. She turned toward Landon. He had leapt down the companion ladder toward her.

"Take to my arm!" He reached out to her as his boots hit the main deck. "Hold on!"

With that, he grabbed her and flung her toward the shelter between two canons secured on the right side of the ship as a barrel clipped the farthest gun, and launched into the air, whirling fiercely. Twisting his body, Landon put himself between Keelan and the flying barrel.

It hit them with the force of a raging bull, then crashed to the deck and broke into pieces.

Keelan gasped in pain and tried to take a breath. A heavy weight prevented any movement. She was face down on the deck.

She craned her neck enough to see Landon's body covering hers. And he wasn't moving.

"Landon!" she cried his name. No movement, no sound. Nothing.

Another voice pierced the gale. She strained to raise her head until finally, Landon was lifted away from her. A sailor dashed up the companion ladder to take the helm along with two others. Gus tossed Landon over his shoulder and Ronnie grabbed Keelan's wrist and pulled her to her feet.

Together, they battled the pitch and roll of the ship to the captain's cabin. Gus dropped Landon on his bed then turned to her, his eyes flashing. "What the blazes did ye think ye were doin' out on that deck? Yer a *lubber*. Ye ain't got any sailin' know-how. Ye just 'bout killed yerself and yer captain, ye witless scamp!"

With clenched fists, Gus advanced upon Keelan like a raging ox. If she hadn't been braced against the cabin wall, she'd have collapsed right there in her boots. As it was, she trembled so violently, her teeth clattered against each other.

Ronnie stepped between Gus and Keelan. "Twas a greenie mistake, sir." His eyes shifted between the two. Gus hadn't been told that Keelan was Landon's wife. They'd decided to wait until after they left Charleston.

In Gus's eyes, she was a young boy, a novice and a liability. Gus was as furious as the tempest outside. "Well, if it wasn't fer this gale, he'd get five lashes from the cat," he spat, shaking his fist.

Ronnie cleared his throat and shifted on his feet. "Mahdi has some knowledge of healing. He can help the ship's sawbones treat the captain. It'll keep him outta the way."

Gus scowled, then shrugged before stomping out. "Go git the surgeon. I'm on watch," he snapped before slamming the door.

Keelan leaned against the cabin wall and squeezed her eyes shut. What had she done? A choked sob escaped her throat, and she fell away from Ronnie's grip and staggered to her husband's bedside. "Landon!"

His wet shirt stuck to his chest like skin. She placed her ear over his heart and closed her eyes, listening.

Dear God, please let him be alive.

Was that a soft, distant heartbeat?

It was.

She examined him, checking for bruises and feeling for broken bones. A small trickle of blood flowed from his ear.

"Let's pull him out of these wet clothes, Miss Keelan," Ronnie whispered, touching her shoulder. "The doc will want to see all of him."

෧෨෩

A DAY LATER, steady rain still pummeled the ship, but the wind and rough seas had abated, somewhat. The sun tried to shove its way through the grey blanket, but the clouds refused it.

The ship's surgeon examined Landon's head, touching a large lump on his temple. "It hasn't changed since last night, a good sign. We'll just have to wait it out," he said, packing up the wooden carrier holding his surgeon's supplies. "That large bruise on his upper back and shoulder may be hiding a broken rib, but it's the hit on the head to worry about."

"How long until he wakes?" Keelan asked, dreading the answer.

"Don't know." He shook his head, turning toward the door. "He may not."

Two days later, Landon still hadn't moved nor made another sound since he'd been placed on his bed; not when they'd removed his clothes, nor when Keelan poured whiskey on the small cut on his temple. Landon didn't even flinch. Putting her head on his chest, she checked yet again for his heartbeat.

Once more, she folded her hands and made her appeal to God for Landon to gain consciousness soon. Her chest flooded with regret. If only she hadn't tried to traverse the deck in the storm. If only she'd stayed below and out of the way, Landon might not have been injured. Why hadn't she simply turned back?

For the thousandth time, she whispered, "Please Landon, love, wake up." She pressed another kiss on his forehead.

This time, as if he'd heard her, Landon's eyelids twitched and he let out a low moan.

"Landon?" Keelan tried to keep her voice level and calm, but she couldn't contain the intertwined notes of relief and concern.

His eyes opened, and he slowly focused his startling blue gaze on her face. His expression changed from wariness to confusion. He lifted his head and winced.

She pressed his shoulders back down. "Go slowly, you're hurt."

"Where am I?" He rubbed his forehead.

"You're in your cabin aboard the *Desire*. You were hit on the head and have been unconscious for two days," she explained.

He attempted to sit up, then grimaced and sunk back to a reclining position. "What happened?"

Keelan bit her lip, then answered, "It was my fault. I shouldn't have come up on deck. A loose barrel hit us during the gale. I... I didn't tie it down correctly. One struck you. Do you remember that?"

"There was a storm?" His hand was over his eyes, as if the light pained him.

He didn't remember the storm? She spoke in a low tone, "Yes. It's blown us quite a ways off course, but Gus said we should arrive in Charleston in a day or two, depending on the wind and the current."

Landon glanced at her from under his hand. "What about Captain O'Brien and Captain Ahern? Did they weather the storm fairly? Have their ships been sighted?"

For a moment, Keelan wasn't sure how to answer. It was impossible for either to be sighted. Both ships were currently bound for Jamaica. Perhaps now wasn't the time to tell her husband his memory was off. She put her hand on his chest. "You're a bit disoriented. You were hit hard."

He stared at her hand, then brushed it away impatiently. Hurt by this, she sat back and regarded him. He was acting... differently.

Something was wrong.

His cool, aloof stare had her heart pounding in her chest and her stomach flipping in trepidation.

"Who are *you*?" he finally asked.

CHAPTER 3

"Answer my question, boy." Landon struggled to his elbows, then pushed himself up further to a sitting position, all the while watching her as if he expected her to stab him in the chest.

How was she supposed to answer that question? As Keelan Hart or as Mahdi? Keelan opened her mouth just as someone knocked.

"Enter." Landon shifted his gaze from her to the door and back. It opened and Gus stuck his head in and grinned.

"Captain! Yer awake! Glad I am to see this, I tell ye." He grinned, then glanced at Keelan. "Mahdi, yer needed in the galley."

She rose on shaky knees. Her mind kept swirling around a single thought:

My husband doesn't recognize me.

Her throat tightened, and she swallowed in an attempt to fend off the tears.

Landon's attention was on his first mate. "Gus, is all well?" He glanced at Keelan. "I had just inquired to the welfare of Conal and Fynn. The boy said there was a storm..."

The boy. That's all she was to him, a boy.

Landon paused, his eyes once again wary as he took in Gus's expression. "What's wrong?"

Gus stepped inside the cabin, his face strangely blank. He opened his mouth, closed it, opened it, then closed it again before lifting a quizzical brow at her. She shrugged, unable to reveal herself to Gus. Landon had insisted that her true identity remain within their small group comprising himself, Daniel and Ronnie. He didn't want to expose the fact that she was a woman to the rest of the crew until they were well away from Charleston and Gampo's spies and reward.

Gus blinked. "Well... er..."

"Out with it, man." Landon swung his feet to the floor then groaned, bracing his hands against the corner walls of the cabin; his eyes closed briefly. When they opened, he focused more or less on Gus.

"Yes. Well ye knows that ye took a hard clubbin' to the noggin, right Cap'n?"

Landon shifted his intense blue gaze to Keelan for a moment. "Yes, Mahdi mentioned that."

Gus shifted his weight and before trying another approach. "What's the last thing ye remember, sir?"

Landon tilted his head, thinking. "Leaving port in Baracoa, to sail for New York."

Gus nodded, pensive. "Which year was that, then?"

Landon started. "Which year?" His eyes narrowed. "The year I returned home to Baracoa, to find my wife had died giving birth to another man's child. *That* year," he said flatly. "1806. And if you want to know the date, it was the twenty-fifth of May."

Keelan fisted her shirt and swallowed. *Over five years ago!*

Gus rubbed the back of his neck and expelled a lungful of breath. He turned on his heel and went to a wall cabinet, opened it and skimmed his thick fingers over several journals before pulling one out. He flipped open the front cover, glanced at it, snapped the book shut and handed it to Landon.

"Ye should have a look at this, Cap'n. Maybe it'll jar loose yer memory," he said in a gentle tone, stepping away.

Landon shot Gus a puzzled look. He opened the book and read aloud, "January *1811?*" He flipped through the pages. "'Tis indeed my hand, but I don't remember writing the words."

He froze, his hand stilled on a page halfway through the book. Brow furrowed, he began to read, "30 May 1811. It is with a heavy heart that we said farewell to Fynn Ahern today. His injuries from the last encounter with Gampo were too severe. As her new captain, Brendan Ahern has taken his father to Baracoa for burial and to arrange repairs for the *Reward*, while Captain O'Brien and I continue ahead to Charleston. It is our decision to keep Captain Ahern's mysterious appointment with Commodore George Grey while our ships are in dry dock. Once the *Reward* can join us, we will continue our route to Philadelphia, then on to New York." Landon's voice cracked, and he cleared his throat.

Keelan's heart went out to him as grief seeped from his eyes. His fingers went slack, and the journal fell to the floor. Dealing with the death of a treasured friend was hard enough the first time. Now, Landon had to relive the anguish of his mentor's passing again. This burden fell on top of the ragged torment raging within him from his wife's betrayal and death, once years in the past, again new and raw as if it happened yesterday.

She retrieved the book from the floor and placed it on the bed, unsure how to comfort him. "Lan—um, Captain Hart…"

He raised his head, misery and sorrow saturated his features like water filled a sponge. "You may go," he said hoarsely. "Gus and I have much to discuss."

Dismissed, Keelan blindly reached for the doorknob. Tears blurred her vision as she slunk from the cabin. She ran below, past the galley and down to the main hold of the ship.

The smell of horses and damp wood assailed her nostrils. Tears streamed down her face. She stumbled to Juliet's stall, heaved the up latch and fell inside. Munching on a mouthful of hay, the mare turned her head toward Keelan and gave her a soft snort. The foal paused a moment from his nursing, then carried on. She ran her hands over Juliet's neck and back before patting the mare's silver flank and sinking to the filthy floor in the far corner of the stall. She hugged her knees to her chest and sobbed.

What had she done? It was her fault the barrels broke loose. If she'd tied them correctly, or at least found someone else who could, Landon would have never been injured. Would his memory return, or would she forever be a stranger to him? A thick sorrow descended and enveloped her, pulling her down into the hopeless dark and taking her future with Landon Hart with it.

A whisper of warm breath on her hair interrupted her misery. "Not now, go away Juliet," she mumbled, keeping her head buried in her arms. Velvety soft lips nuzzled her ear, and she shook her head. "Leave me be." Another huff and more nuzzling on her neck had her opening her eyes.

Two black, spidery legs wobbled near her right foot. Keelan raised her head. The soft brown eyes of Juliet's foal contemplated her with a calm interest.

"Well, hello, young one," she whispered. "My, but aren't you a handsome little man?"

His upper lip twitched, and he nudged her forehead.

She sighed. "I suppose you're right. I should return to my duties."

A light whistling attracted his attention, and the foal turned his head toward the stall door. Daniel stepped inside and placed a water bucket on the floor. He started when he saw her. "Miss Keelan?" he whispered. "Are you all right?" He stepped over and squatted in front of her, his eyes hooded with concern.

"Landon woke up."

He grinned, the smile lines from the corners of his eyes creased to the silver hair of his temples. "Wonderful news, that." He tilted his head, once again serious. "But why are you so mournful?"

Her chin quivered, and she wiped her nose with her sleeve. "He doesn't recognize me."

Daniel's gray eyes widened. "He doesn't?"

"His memories from the past five years are gone." She swallowed as her voice faltered, "He doesn't know who I am. It's as if we never met. In fact, he doesn't even seem to *like* me."

Daniel touched her hand lightly. "Did you tell him you were his wife?"

She shook her head. "How, when in his mind, he'd only recently learned that his wife was not only dead but also an adulteress? Besides, Gus was with us in the cabin."

She stared at Daniel's hand, draped across his knee. The dye on his skin was still a shade darker; hers had started to fade. "Daniel, he didn't remember that Uncle Fynn had been killed. Gus made him read his journal, and he had to relive the pain of Fynn's loss again."

Daniel gave her a sad shake of his head and rose to his feet. He held out his hand, and she accepted it, allowing him to pull her up. "It might take time for his memories to return. Be patient," he said.

She shrugged and nodded. What more could she do?

⚜

KEELAN WENT to the galley and helped Marcel prepare for the next meal. With the seas calmer, he could rouse the fire and heat a large kettle of water. They made Hoppin' John for the crew. She also made scones for Landon and his officers.

That part of her work done, Keelan wandered up to the main deck. The crew gathered in a circle near the main mast. Before she made it to the edge of the group, the *clash* and *ching* of metal against metal told her someone was sparring with blades. Unable to see past the crewmen, she headed toward the companion ladder near where Landon and Gus relaxed at the helm.

Landon, while upright, leaned heavily against the rail, pale and drawn. Even so, his keen azure gaze trapped hers for a moment. She caught her breath, hoping. He shifted his attention to the duelers. A heaviness pressed on her shoulders and chest. He still didn't recognize her.

She meant nothing to him.

When she topped the third step, she could see over the heads of the sailors. Daniel and Ronnie circled each other, sabers up. Ronnie swung his weapon. Daniel was still and fluid at the same time. A flash of silver followed by a strident, metallic clash blocked Ronnie's strike. Ronnie parried and struck out again, only to end up with the tip of Daniel's sword at his chin.

The men roared and clapped. Ronnie grinned and shook his head while Daniel raised his sword and gave him a spry salute. When Daniel lowered his weapon, he caught sight of Keelan.

Ronnie raised his sword. "Let's have another go, Mr. Kahlil, what do you say?" Ronnie used Daniel's alias, keeping with the charade Daniel and Keelan had to play.

"I have a suggestion instead, Mr. Ahern," Daniel replied, nodding toward Keelan. "Mahdi has been negligent in his training of late. It would do him good to exercise his sword arm a bit. Mahdi?"

Ronnie's eyes widened, "But, sir—"

Daniel took out a handkerchief and mopped his forehead. "It's quite all right. Mahdi and I used to train together every morning. He should be an adequate sparring partner for you." He gestured to Keelan, then paused as if he might reconsider. "That is, if the wounds have healed enough on your back?" His forehead creased with concern. He'd forgotten about her still healing lashes, but they were mostly closed now.

Gampo and his men had stolen Landon's cargo, then kidnapped her from her uncle's Charleston town house. One of Gampo's men had whipped her for refusing his advances. That was close to a month ago. Landon had asked her to sail away with him that night, as his wife, and she'd joyfully accepted. She glanced up at her husband again. He simply stared at her, waiting for her to respond to Daniel's challenge, nothing in his gaze but a mild interest.

Their first meeting had occurred after a sparring session between her and Daniel. She'd dressed much as she was now, in boy's clothes and boots. Her heart lifted a bit. Perhaps this exercise might nudge his memory of that day. She shifted her gaze back to Daniel and smiled. "I believe they've healed enough for a small test."

The men roared with approval and parted for her to enter the circle.

"But..." Ronnie looked from Daniel to Keelan. "Mahdi is... is...."

Daniel lowered his brows in warning, lest Ronnie forget himself and expose her.

Ronnie's eyes widened. "I'm a head taller and two stones heavier! Tis not a fair fight!" he blurted.

Daniel caught Keelan's eye and the corner of his mouth twitched. "You're right, it's not a fair fight." He handed her his sword. "But I'm sure Mahdi will go easy on you at the beginning."

The men guffawed and Ronnie's ears reddened. He reached up and scratched the back of his shoulder then, still dubious, gave a slight shrug of acquiescence.

Keelan attempted a few practice swings to test the elasticity of the skin across her shoulders. An uncomfortable pull stretched against the gently healed wounds, but nothing painful. As long as she could move fast enough to block and pay, she should at least be able to hold her own. She increased the speed and made a figure eight. Nothing stung or pained her, so she stopped and nodded to Daniel. "Feels good enough."

The men were silent a moment before a sailor called out, "Sixpence on the boy!"

"Which one?"

"The Persian!"

"I'll put six on Ronnie!"

With that, there were more bets and jovial taunting among the crew. Keelan raised her sword in a salute, and Ronnie did the same. Both began circling. Ronnie made the first move, lunging half-heartedly at her. Keelan stepped aside, batted his blade down, spun and slapped the flat of her blade across his back as he stumbled past.

The men laughed and continued to toss out jibes and bets. She faced him again. Ronnie's lips were in a thin line and his face reddened at the good-natured cheers and jeers from the men. His internal struggle was well-played out on his face. He wanted to win, but she was a female and every instinct in every bone in his body told him to protect her—not attack her.

"C'mon Ronnie, lad!"

"Yer a head taller and a stone or two heavier, remember? Put yer weight into it!"

Ronnie raised his brows at her, asking for permission to increase his advance. In response, she attacked, forcing him to move swiftly in order to parry. His surprise turned into intense determination as his swings became faster and harder. The two lunged, swung, blocked and parried for several more minutes until both were panting from the exertion.

Ronnie was stronger, but predictable. All she had to do was faint to the left to pull him off balance, kick his feet out from under him, and she'd win. However, she needed Ronnie's help and protection. He seemed like a good lad, but she'd met him only a week ago, and couldn't take the risk she'd wound his youthful pride so much that he'd lash out later and reveal her disguise or refuse to assist her and Daniel when they needed him.

Keelan slowed down her pace and brought her weapon up in a diagonal slash, allowing Ronnie the opportunity to block and disarm her, which he did.

She raised her hands. "I yield."

The men cheered and crowded him, slapping him on the back, but he caught her gaze and his eyes narrowed, catching the tiniest lift of her chin in response. She'd not embarrass him in front of the men, but neither would she lie to him.

Keelan couldn't stop herself from glancing back to the helm. Did it work? Landon frowned at her. It hadn't. Not only had it not jolted his memory, but now he looked angry. What had she done to raise his ire this time?

The activity had winded her and a fine sweat covered her brow and face. She absently reached up and removed the faded cloth from her head and used it to wipe her face and neck. Landon whirled away from her, hands braced on the rail, his attention shifting to the horizon, effectively turning his back on her both physically and emotionally.

She was more alone now than she'd been in her entire life.

CHAPTER 4

The belly of the *Desire* creaked and groaned. It was dusk and the last vestiges of the sun's rays skittered over the wall opposite the porthole as the ship rose and fell with the rolling ocean. Keelan dipped a rag into the shallow bowl of tepid water and rubbed it over her face, neck and arms, wiping away the grit of dried salt spray. She studied the top of her hand, then craned her head and peered at the back of her shoulder. The stain had definitely faded. She glanced at the small bottle of dye near the bowl. She'd have to reapply it before they returned to port.

The thought of another application had her wrinkling her nose. The dye had been made from a mixture of molasses, black walnut hulls, and a partially burned hog carcass. The odor wasn't unpleasant as much as out of place. Would the crew wonder why she smelled like a burned ham, or would they not think on it, since she worked in the galley?

Hopefully, the latter.

She let her shoulders fall and huffed out a short sigh. Best to get it done; she'd put it off long enough. She pulled the stopper from the bottle of dye and paused. Mrs. Schoen, a tavern keeper's wife and a part of Fynn's network of folk helping slaves escape to freedom, had rubbed the dye on Keelan's face and shoulders the first time.

There was no way for her to spread the stain evenly over her face by herself without a mirror. Thankfully, Landon had one in their cabin. If he was still on the aft deck talking with Gus, she'd have plenty of time to borrow it. She would be in and out before he returned for bed.

"Is The Whistling Pig Tavern still our Charleston contact point?" Landon needed to know how much things had changed over the past five years. It seemed that, other than dates of landfall and the value of cargo, much had remained the same except for the battle that had cost Fynn his life.

And a relationship with a woman named Keelan Grey, according to Ronnie.

"Aye," Gus said, packing his pipe and lighting it. "If any runaways made it there, then Mr. Schoen will have them hid away beneath the tavern for us, or up in the attic."

"That makes things easier." It was with a sense of relief that he remembered the friendly German tavern keeper and his wife. This situation was bloody annoying, not recognizing a face when he should. Thankfully, Gus spent the day at his shoulder, whispering names in his ear so the crew would not guess his recent affliction.

Five years.

It had been five years since he'd sailed from Baracoa, a widower. He'd been a fool to take a wife, he knew that now. She'd been both beautiful and the daughter of a ship's captain. She knew of a sailor's life and accepted him just the same. He'd been convinced he'd found a wife who'd understood the call of the sea, the months of separation...

When he'd made port after nearly a year and came home to a

cold hearth and tight-lipped townsfolk, he'd sought out the priest to inquire the location of his wife. The priest led him to a gravesite where she rested. He'd fallen to his knees in grief and shock. It was many minutes before he read the markings on the stone. Both his wife and her child had died of fever a week after the child was born.

The month prior to his return.

He'd been gone a year.

Even an idiot would be able to deduce that she'd gotten pregnant *after* he went to sea. The grief of loss coupled with the pain of her betrayal had been almost too much for him to bear. He'd made a vow that day.

Never again.

Never again would he give away his heart. Never again would he marry.

Gus gestured to the stern, then took a pull on his pipe. He blew the smoke out in a long, thin stream. "Well, at least ye still know the difference between the bow of a ship and the stern. 'Tis a start." He chuckled good naturedly at his own joke.

Landon glowered at his first mate before turning his gaze back to the wake swirling and gurgling behind the ship. "If my head didn't still pound harder than a smithy at an anvil, I'd box your ears just for thinking that thought." He sipped from his tankard, then stared into its depths. "I usually know every man hired to serve on my ship. Now, at least a quarter of the men are strangers."

His mind drifted to Fynn's son, Ronnie. "In my last memory of Ronnie, he was six inches shorter and had a voice like a nun."

"And knobby legs and a penchant for disaster," Gus added with a laugh.

"Remember when he raced McAllister to the tip of the topgallant brace and back?" Landon chuckled.

Gus slapped his knee and stretched out his thick legs before crossing his ankles. "Aye, I do! Like a scrawny monkey, he was."

CHLOE FLOWERS

He puffed on his pipe. "McAllister gave up halfway through. He knew he'd lost."

"Seeing Ronnie, now as a growing young man, finally forced me to accept that I've been robbed of my memories from the past five years." Landon mumbled, almost to himself.

"Has anything come back to ye?" Gus blew a ring of smoke and watched it drift away.

"Not yet," Landon said. "Not entirely. You seem unconcerned with it. I have to admit, it vexes me beyond my patience." Bloody inconvenient was what it was and unnerving. He felt weak and helpless, and he hated it.

Gus struck a match and relit his pipe. "Well, lad, I've seen me share of carnage and mystery all involving men's lives and deaths. Things happen sometimes ye can't explain away." He stared up at the sky for a moment, then continued. "Once, I chatted with a man in a pub in Cadiz. He kept having furious dreams of drowning and burning at the same time. The dreams invaded his head both day and night. At last, it was time for his ship to sail; he stood on her deck as she was leaving port, seeing the same images over and over in 'is head until he lost his mind and dove overboard. He swam ashore and walked back to town. He said the horrible images left his head, and he felt calm, content. He signed on with another merchant the next day. Never had them dreams again."

Gus puffed on his pipe a moment before he continued. "He found out later that the ship he'd abandoned had been seized by Tripolitan pirates. They'd taken all they could hold, then scuppered the ship. Set charges to blow up her magazines with the crew still tied to the lines and masts. If the explosion didn't kill the crew, the water did when the ship went under." He locked his gaze to the heavens again and sighed.

"It's near impossible to try to figure out how yer head works, Cap'n. I've seen men clobbered hard enough that they forgot their names and never remembered them again. I've seen other's wake up the next day fine as sea mist." Gus turned his pipe upside down and tapped it over the rail, sending the coals into the sea.

Landon stared at the glossy water moving behind his ship. "Images seep into my mind like the smoke from your pipe... one moment a swirling shape, the next... a wisp of nothing."

"Give it time, Cap'n. Give it time. You never know, something familiar may happen that opens the door."

Landon leaned back in his chair, pensive. His mind was blocked by a curtain; all he needed was a strong enough breeze to move it. Today, when Ronnie and the young Persian had sparred near the helm, something—a movement, a color, a fragrance—had invaded that dark closed off place in his head. He'd been hopeful his mind would open, and he'd remember. Nothing had happened. Nothing at all. He was left with a twisting sensation in his gut telling him that he'd missed something, he just didn't know what.

CHAPTER 5

Keelan strolled into the galley, bucket in hand. "Should I pour some water into the captain's pitcher?" she asked Marcel, already knowing the answer.

"*Oui*. He will expect it," the old cook answered, not looking up from his task.

Gus told her that he and Landon had decided to keep his memory loss a secret from the crew; they'd agreed that this was no time to lose the confidence of the men. Even now, British ships and privateers prowled the waters, seeking a prize like the *Desire*. This ship and its crew had to remain unified and strong.

"These are good men when they have faith in their ship and her captain," Gus had said. "We can't give 'em reason to doubt."

Keelan carried the bucket half-filled with fresh rain water to Landon's cabin, the bottle of dye tucked into her boot. Daniel informed her that Landon and Gus were currently talking near the stern, enjoying a tankard of ale where no one could eavesdrop. They were reading through the most recent journals, with the hope that something would pull Landon's memory to the present. It couldn't happen too soon.

Keelan kicked the door closed and hurried to the deep bowl

Landon had placed for her near the water closet. She pulled the bottle from her boot and emptied it into the basin and then added some water. She found the mirror in one of Landon's desk drawers next to his shaving supplies.

Beside the mirror sat a small box. She stroked it. Inside, wrapped in a piece of silk, was her wedding ring. It had been Landon's grandmother's. The night Landon had knelt in front of her and pledged his love and fidelity, he had gifted her that ring. With her lifelong mentor Daniel, and her brother Conal as witnesses, she and Landon performed an ancient handfast ceremony, pledging their hearts and lives to each other. Afterward, Landon had promised to marry her in a church as soon as they made port.

Opening the box, she removed the ring and put it on her finger. The cool metal warmed to her skin. She clutched it to her chest, hating and loving the ache it caused. Landon *loved* her. Somewhere deep inside the recesses of his wounded mind, there was a bone deep love for her. There had to be a way to pull it out into the light once again. The sparkle of the rubies and diamonds glittered in the dim light of the cabin. Landon had carried the ring with him the day they were to be married in Harbour Town, but of course after Conal went missing, the nuptials were delayed.

If Landon didn't regain his memories, it might never happen at all.

She pulled out the mirror and propped it up beside the basin. That accomplished, she tugged off Landon's old linen shirt and tossed it on the bed, then unlaced the leather corset that bound her breasts. She pulled off the cloth covering her hair and dropped it into the dye. Her natural auburn locks had begun to emerge as the stain faded, prompting her to keep her head covered. It seemed to help with the disguise as well. The crew never questioned the claim that she and Daniel were Persians. The cloth also helped keep the sun from burning her neck and scalp.

The ship creaked and moaned as the wind gripped her sails. Sometimes, the *Desire* seemed to act like an old dog, groaning, sighing and growling. Her timbers, spars, and lines whined with every movement of the sea. Keelan actually enjoyed listening to the ship chatter her condition as she slid across the water. It soothed her, as if they were both mourning Landon's affliction. They were in this together, she and the *Desire*. And together they would bring him back.

It didn't take long to rub the stain into her arms, chest and neck. She couldn't reach as far back behind her shoulders as Mrs. Schoen had done and prayed her administrations were enough to cover the necessary areas. The slashes where Gampo's former first mate had marked her back were gently healed, but she avoided them as she applied the dye over her shoulders.

Her face would be the hardest to stain. Propping the mirror at a better angle, she reminded herself to use steady, even strokes. A streak or blotch on her face would quickly expose her charade to the crew.

She dipped the rag in the basin and squeezed it as best she could, then leaned closer to Landon's mirror and carefully wiped it across her forehead. She repeated the slow, even swipes across her cheeks and nose, then chin before blotting with a dry rag and repeating the process. The lantern swayed in a slow sweep, shifting shadows and light. She would celebrate the day she could put away the disguise and finally be herself again.

Moving on to her hair, she pulled the dye-soaked cloth from her scalp down to the ends. At first, she'd been a bit wary of living aboard a ship. Nausea had gripped her stomach the first few days, but Marcel's ginger root had helped settle it. After a few weeks, she'd become accustomed to the inhalation and the exhalation of the *Desire,* as the ship cut through the water. The motion of the sea no longer made her queasy. The old Landon would have been proud of her for that. She paused. The old Landon loved her. The new Landon barely noticed her. To him, along with the rest of the crew, she was the Persian boy, Mahdi.

The memory of their moonlit garden dance drifted through her thoughts. It had been the night of her cousin's ball. The moon was luminous enough to cast shadows in the garden. She'd ventured out for fresh air and to escape a suitor and his clumsy attempts at dancing, which had been painful for her toes.

Landon had pulled her into a waltz and it had been just the two of them. His hand against her waist had been distracting, his words even more so. He was witty and charming, and before she knew what was happening, she'd been goaded into a bet that she couldn't initiate a kiss with passion. Of course, she accepted; she'd never been able to refuse a challenge, however foolhardy.

She'd kissed him, and time stopped. The moon quit pulling the tide, the earth ceased spinning, and the breeze froze in the sky. Landon stirred a fire in her heart that heated her entire body, and all she wanted was for his arms to hold her forever.

She paused and lowered the rag. She wanted the old Landon back. She *needed* him back, and she wasn't about to stand idly and wait for him. There had to be something she could do to help him regain his memory. Daniel might have some ideas. When she finished here, she'd seek him out. They'd form a plan.

The light in the cabin had dimmed with the approach of evening; she turned up the lantern a tiny bit, then brought the mirror close to her face for an inspection nearer the light. There were no uneven blotches. She nodded in satisfaction. Once she pulled back her hair and covered it, all signs of the fiery tresses would be extinguished.

She shifted the mirror for a better view of the side of her neck, then caught a movement in the glass. She twirled. Landon stood with his hand still on the latch of the closed door, jaw slightly open.

"Landon!" His name fell from her mouth before she could

stop it. Her heart pounded hard in her chest and for a moment, she froze.

His eyes widened and traveled from her face to her bare chest, then over her boy's breeches and boots, then back up again. "What in God's name...." He clenched his jaw and in two strides closed the space between them. His movement finally broke her temporary paralysis, and she lunged for her shirt still draped over their bed. *His* bed now, since he had no memory of ever sharing it with her.

He reached her before she could take a second step, grabbed her arms and pushed her against the wall of the cabin. His crystalline irises flashed in anger. "Who the hell are you?" His gaze raked once more past her stained face, neck and chest to her naked breasts and pale stomach.

"And no more lies," he growled.

If he expected her to shrink in fear, he'd be disappointed. She lifted her chin and glared back at him best as she could, considering the top of her head barely reached his jaw. His palms burned the skin of her arms, and she fought to keep herself from melting into him.

He grabbed her wrist in a painful vise and twisted it up between them and in front of her face. "You can begin by telling me why you have stolen a family heirloom that once belonged to my grandmother," he ground the words out through clenched teeth.

The ring! She'd forgotten it was on her finger. Her throat constricted, not allowing her to swallow. He could have her punished for thievery. If only she could be certain the truth would jar his memory, she'd tell him everything.

But... what if it didn't?

One thing was certain, if he believed she was trying to steal from him, not only would she lose any chance of gaining his trust, but he'd probably order the quartermaster to impose on her a harsh punishment. The wounds on her back from the last lashing she received had not fully healed. She'd not survive another.

There'd be no more tiptoeing around the truth, then.

She met his hot blue glare with her own of green fire. "I am Keelan O'Brien Hart. Your *wife*."

Landon fell back as if he'd been shot. His face paled and his lips moved but made no sound. "Impossible," he finally whispered hoarsely. He backed into the edge of the bed, then sat, still staring.

"It's entirely possible," she stated, pulling at the shirt he'd trapped beneath his hip when he sat.

"Did you say *O'Brien*? As in Conal O'Brien?" He peered at her and cocked his head to the side, then once again raked his gaze over her head to foot, stuttering when it reached her breasts.

She tugged harder at the shirt, but he seemed oblivious to her struggle. "Yes, O'Brien. I'm Conal's sister."

Landon's eyes narrowed then. "I know every member of Conal's family. He has no sister named Keelan."

She finally forfeited her quest for the shirt and stepped back, crossing her arms over her chest, both in irritation and a small amount of modesty. As his wife, she wasn't opposed to revealing her naked body to him, but this particular situation confused things more than a bit.

"I was taken from my crib as a baby and raised by a British commodore and his wife. You mentioned his name when you read aloud a page of your journal the day you awoke. Commodore George Grey." She studied his face. A glimmer of acknowledgment, a tiny light of recognition flickering in his eyes, would give her hope. But there was nothing.

He pressed his lips together and leaned back. "That sounds rather outlandish." He nodded toward the ring.

"It's the truth," she snapped, unable to hide her disappointment.

"Prove it."

"Papa—Commodore Grey, gave me a signet ring and half a locket with a miniature of my and Conal's, father. The ring had a family crest with four lions, a shaft of wheat and a knight's helm." She silently prayed the information would help him remember something.

Anything.

Landon shrugged. "Show me the ring."

She fidgeted and edged toward the tall boy, then jerked open a drawer and removed another shirt. "Conal has it."

Silence. "How convenient."

She glared at him before she shrugged into the shirt. "Ask Daniel. He witnessed our vows."

"Who's Daniel?" He crossed his arms over his broad chest, making the muscles in his arms bulge and her mouth go dry.

She groaned in exasperation. "Daniel is a loyal servant who's been with me all my life. He's disguised as Kahlil on your ship. He tends the horses." Her story was starting to resemble an elaborate fictional tale, even to her ears. How could she prove she told the truth when the truth sounded outrageous, even to her?

He sat back and leaned against the cabin wall. "Why didn't Gus tell me that you were my wife?"

She inwardly groaned. Could her stomach sink any further? All she could do was shake her head and tell the truth. "He doesn't yet know. We decided to wait until we left Charleston before we told any of the crew."

He snorted a sarcastic laugh. "Of course, how convenient for you, *again*." He flicked his hand at her. "Why this elaborate disguise?" Ice blue eyes raked her, sending a chill across her shoulders. "I can think of no reason for it, except deceit." He lowered his chin and captured her gaze, his eyes cold and unyielding. "And believe me, my sweet, I am well-experienced when it comes to a woman's knack for duplicity."

He reached for her wrist and pulled her until she stood between his knees at the edge of the bed. She searched his face for the tiniest flicker of recognition, but it remained impassive. He pulled her closer still and studied her face. She did her best to meet his gaze confidently, but she still blinked first. He leaned back and smirked.

When he spoke, his voice was deadly soft, "I don't believe you. I don't recognize your face, and I would have *never* married again. I *will never* marry again."

Who was this man? "I have no reason to lie," she whispered. Tears burned the backs of her eyes.

She held her breath as he turned her hand over and touched the ring with his fingertips. "No?"

Keelan ground her teeth together and yanked off the ring and slapped it into his waiting palm. He slid it on his little finger where it went no further than the first knuckle.

She started to step back, but he stopped her by capturing her wrist once again. He ran his fingers across her palm, sending shivers up her arm. He slid the shirt cuff up and caressed the tender skin on her inner forearm. Her pulse quickened, as it always did when his fingers touched her. Her eyelids fluttered closed, replaying the scene in her mind from their first kiss in her aunt's garden.

Was he remembering it, too? Dare she even hope?

His other hand splayed on the flat of her stomach and she trembled. The need within her awakened and began to swirl in her belly beneath the warmth of his palm. She could barely breathe as he stroked her hip, then up her ribs to the outer curve of her breast.

Please. Remember me. Please.

She almost reached for his hand. She loved his touch, his warmth and the passion he stirred deep within her own body. A low throb of desire pulsed within her, and she wanted more than anything to feel the heat and fire of Landon Hart's lovemaking. Her fingers ached to twist in his long dark hair. Her palms tingled, wanting to move over his chest and bump over the hard ridges of his stomach.

A powerful aura radiated from Landon, and when he was near, its energy drew her in and surged through her like a cyclone. It both bound them and pulsed through them like life's blood, linking their hearts, their souls and their desires. It warmed her now, like a radiant heat. His scent filled her nostrils, and she breathed him in. Her arms ached to hold him and pull him into her. She wanted to make love with him until they both flew high up to that place of ecstasy where suns explode and stars surge through the universe.

Was he remembering, too?

Remember me.

The warmth of his palm covered her breast and her nipples hardened. A hungry ache swirled in her lower belly. Her lids flickered open, hoping. She had her hands in his hair. His eyes flamed with desire, his mouth parted for kissing. He wanted her as much as she wanted him. His shirt laces were undone, as if he had been prepared to disrobe when he entered earlier. The muscles of his chest rippled with the movement of his hand. She searched his face. Did he remember? The blue depths of his irises seemed too shallow, too light. The dark pools of passion she used to fall into were not there.

His expression shifted; his mouth curled up.

And her heart broke.

His slow, lusty smile dropped the final stone. Now, she felt sullied and cheap. Tears welled in her eyes; she squeezed them shut and struggled to gather her composure.

She stilled his roving hand with hers. "Tell me," she asked, her voice hoarse and weak. "Where did we meet?"

"What?" His eyes were still on her chest.

"Where did we first kiss?" She pulled his hand away, ignoring his slight look of surprise. She stepped back as he reached for her again. He grasped her hand and brought her palm to his lips, like he'd done in the garden weeks ago. For a moment, hope surged anew.

"If we are truly married, then perhaps my memory will return if I exercise my husbandly duties," he murmured.

If we are truly married. *If.*

His hand fell as she stepped farther away. "You don't believe me." Her hands shook as she fought to tie her shirt. She had exposed that tenderest strand of hope way too soon. It was like an exposed nerve, and Landon's words sliced right through it, leaving her raw and jagged.

He leaned back on the bed and rested on his elbows. "Well, I suppose I could ask Daniel, that *loyal* servant of yours, who would probably lie for you a thousand times if you asked in the proper manner."

Her face burned at his insinuations.

She finished tying her shirt and glanced toward the door. That deep baritone she had come to adore now grated against her ears. She couldn't stay and endure any more shards flying from his mouth. This man, whom she no longer knew, wounded her deeply. She wanted to grasp his broad shoulders and shake him. She wanted to demand he remember her... remember *them*.

Reason made her pause. Her life and Daniel's depended upon their identities remaining hidden. If Landon exposed them in his current state, she and Daniel would be in danger. She had no choice. She had to avoid raising his ire, no matter how much he deserved a sharp dressing down. Gritting her teeth, she finally met his mocking gaze.

Ignoring his cocky grin, she paused for a calming breath before she spoke. "You wanted me to explain my disguise. It's necessary to keep me safe. Gampo placed a steep price upon my head in Charleston. Whether you remember it or not, you should know that I am in this disguise at *your* recommendation. You and Daniel designed this charade to keep me safe."

She spread her palms in surrender. "Despise me if you must,

but take care before you reveal my real identity, because if you do, my life will be in immediate danger and you will place Daniel's life in jeopardy as well." She turned and grasped the door handle.

"Where are you going, *wife*? It's late."

A tight ache clamped her chest, squeezing hard. Even breathing hurt. "I'll find someplace to sleep where I won't have to worry about being accosted by leering men," she snapped, unable to bite her tongue in time.

"But didn't you just try to tell me that you're my wife? If that you are, then you should share my cabin."

There was that word again.

If.

"I wouldn't be comfortable sharing a bed with a... stranger." She almost choked over those words. If only he would remember her!

"A stranger? But are we not *married*?" He leaned back on the bed and rested on his elbows. "Do we not already *know* each other... in every sense of the word?"

A heavy sadness enveloped her and the weight of it pressed down on her shoulders. She couldn't meet his gaze; if it was mocking, her heart would shatter even more. "You're not a stranger to me, Landon. But, as long as I am a stranger to you, I cannot share your bed." She opened the door to leave.

"So, you're stealing my shirt?"

Keelan gripped the door handle as hard as she could, otherwise she would have used her fist to bloody his pompous nose. She paused and glared at him over her shoulder.

"This is *my* shirt, Captain. You're sitting on the one you had *given* me." *Off your back, as a matter of fact.* With that, she opened the door and swung it shut with as much force as she could muster, and felt better for it.

Even with the door closed, his voice found her ears. "If I notice anything else missing, you can bet I'll take great, great pleasure in searching you first, *Mahdi*."

CHAPTER 6

How could they possibly pull off any type of plan when there wasn't even a whisper of a breeze? Keelan helped the crew over the next few hours. They lowered each sail and soaked it with water, to force the fibers to expand and hold as much wind as possible. After Keelan had done her part, she sat on one of the water barrels and observed as her husband stood with legs braced, tall, broad and commanding and divulged his plan to the crew. The men grinned broadly and clapped their hands in approval, then listened intently as Gus gave each their instructions.

She shaded her eyes and noted that a launch and a small cutter from the *Glory* continued to take turns lashing the anchor to the boat, rowing ahead to the length of the extended chain then dropping it to wait for the big ship to haul to them by weighing in the anchor. As the *Desire* had been doing for the past three days, they repeated the entire process, over and over.

She moved her attention to the closest British ship. Her stomach twisted; they had attached an anchor to each end of the hawser which passed through a pipe on each side of the bow, allowing the crew to warp the ship ahead continuously, one anchor being carried forward while the other held on to the ocean bottom. The crew did their best to cut the distance to the *Glory*. How long would it be before the British were within firing range?

"I have a task for you."

She jumped before she could prevent it.

Landon's mouth twitched as he handed her the glass. He gestured to the left side of the ship. "We are windward, that is upwind, of the Brits and the *Glory*, meaning any squall off the coast will hit us first. I want you to study the shoreline. Look for gulls or pelicans," he said.

"Why?" She put the glass up to her eye. A coastline of tan sand gave way to pale, shaggy clumps of grass. Farther away, a verdant green line of pine trees spiked toward the sky.

"When the wind picks up, you'll be able to tell by the way the birds react to it."

At her quizzical look, he explained further. "Instead of flapping their wings to move, they'll be able to face the shore and hover in place while they scan the water for prey. It'll seem as if they've been suspended from a string. Understand?"

She lowered the glass. "Yes, I understand." Turning, her gaze collided with Landon's throat. His ties were still undone, and she froze. Couldn't the man at least cover himself in the presence of a woman? She lifted her gaze to connect with his lusty leer.

"My offer still stands, you know." His voice, low and gravelly soft, melted some things inside her while setting others aflame.

"Offer?" Her focus was affixed to the curves of his mouth and the light stubble coating his jaw. She resisted the temptation to trace that small scar on his chin.

"The one to exercise my husbandly duties in a strident attempt to prod my memory back to the present." His eyes drifted down the length of her form.

Heaven knew she wanted that more than her next breath. If only... she closed her eyes and forced her heart to be silent. Her voice came out as a whispered hiss, emotion tangling in her throat. "And my reply still stands as well, Captain Hart. Until you remember how we met, or our first kiss, I'll continue to decline. I won't play a strumpet to a husband who doesn't remember loving me."

He laughed, then shrugged. "Then we are at an impasse until your 'brother,' Conal, can confirm he witnessed our hand-fast vows."

The urge to roll her eyes was overwhelming. It was ironic, really. After they'd met, it had taken quite some time before she had believed Landon's intentions were honorable enough to trust him with her heart. There'd been too many warnings about men of the sea and their aversion to commitments to anyone but their captain and their vessel. She'd suspected that he was using her as a target for his weapons of charm and charisma. She'd tried to resist his appeal and the lure of his spirit, but something more had drawn them close, an unseen essence pulled them together.

Landon had shifted from a free-roving bachelor to a man who earnestly bound himself to her. When that happened, she'd been able to let down her shield and open her heart and trust him.

No, the irony wasn't lost on her. Oh, how the tides had turned.

Laughing, he started toward the helm, speaking over his shoulder. "Let me know immediately when the wind picks up."

Keelan made a face at her husband's back. "Aye, Captain," she muttered through clenched teeth. She plopped her bottom back on the barrel. How did she fall in love with such a conceited, lewd, arrogant scoundrel? The tall, broad shouldered man strode toward the helm like a panther prowling the jungle. His shirt was untucked but beneath it he had a lean tapered waist and strong muscular thighs. He was a handsome devil, to be sure, but he was not the Landon she'd fallen in love with. This Landon Hart was a different man. Is this who he'd been five years ago? A bitter dandy? Derisive? Wary?

Cold?

The pain in her heart stole her breath. Where was the man

who'd fought pirates to save her? Where was the man who'd used his body as a shield to protect her? Even when she'd initially chosen another's offer of marriage over his, Landon had still returned for her and persuaded her to sail away with him. He'd not allowed his pride to stand in the way of his heart's desire, then.

A quick movement beneath one of the guns drew her attention. Soon, a scruffy ear and a pair of green eyes peeked around a wheel as Louis crouched low and followed every move she made with those yellow-green eyes.

"You," she said. "You're another one who's too proud to let down your guard."

She reached into her pocket, pulled out a small chunk of cheese and broke off a bead-sized bite, then tossed it toward the cat. He pounced on the tidbit and promptly ate it, then sat up and stared at her.

"Oh, no." She shook her head. "If you want more, you'll have to ask nicely." She pinched off another morsel and held it out.

Louis stared at her a moment, warily twitching his tail back and forth. After a moment, he rose and slunk toward her, like a tiger stalking prey. Keelan kept her perch on the barrel and waited. She dropped her hand down and let the cheese roll on her palm. When he reached the barrel, Louis studied her a moment before he stretched his front paws up the side until he could swat the cheese to the deck.

She smiled and wrinkled her nose at him. "See? I'm not as horrid as you think I am." She broke off another small piece and nibbled it.

Louis licked his lips and sat down to contemplate her words. Or, more likely, wait to see if she would offer him another bite. When she ignored him, he sauntered around to the other side of the barrel and sat down once more. Staring.

Still, she did not acknowledge him. He twitched his tail, impatiently. Either stay and look from afar or move closer. Decision made, he leapt up to the barrel and rubbed his face on her arm, then sat and gave her a soft yowl. She fed him another tiny piece, but didn't try to touch him.

He wolfed it down, then licked his chops. "So, the way to a cat's heart is through his stomach, just like a man, is that it?" She turned her attention to the helm.

To Landon.

Strong shoulders. Powerful thighs. Large hands that caressed her skin as gently as a feather. An easy laugh and a good heart. A *good* heart, not a lecherous one.

Landon Hart might be cocky and self-centered on the outside, but inside... *inside*, he believed in doing the right thing over the easy thing. He didn't fear adversity or hard choices. Yes, he was proud and stubborn, but he was strong enough to admit when he was wrong.

That was *her* Landon.

But this one... if only she could find a way to help him remember *her*. Something inside her chest hardened then surged, filling her with a granite resolve. Landon hadn't given up on her when she'd rejected him. So, she'd not give up on him. He fell in love with her once. He could fall in love with her again.

She'd make sure of it.

KEELAN SIGHED and raised the spyglass to her eye. So far... nothing. How many hours had it been? Three? Four?

There! A lone pelican caught her attention. It hovered above the waves for a few seconds and then plunged into the water. Is that the sign Landon wanted? She hopped off her barrel and headed toward the helm.

THE SOFT BREATH of the sea breeze gently caressed Keelan's cheek as it loosened a defiant curl from the ribbon tied at her nape. She absentmindedly slipped it behind her ear while she waited in silence with the rest of the crew. Beyond the natural sounds of the sea and the creaking and groaning of the *Desire*, a thick stillness coated the deck. The long boat had already been hoisted and re-stowed in anticipation of the wind's arrival, the signs of which Keelan had alerted Landon a short while ago. Every crew member stood at the ready, awaiting orders from Captain Hart.

They did not have long to wait. A sudden gust hit the ship, snapping the loosened canvas like a whip. At Landon's sharp bark, the men sprang into action. With a sudden lurch, the ship tipped toward the ocean as the men below rolled the guns across the gun deck fast to port. Keelan gripped the pail of salt water.

"Drop canvas!"

The *Desire's* sails were quickly lowered to the deck surface and there was a jump to action as sailors tossed buckets of sea water on the sheets to re-soak the threads. When the dampened sails were re-hoisted, they would capture as much wind as possible.

The *Desire* jerked and rocked and Keelan refilled her bucket. She glanced at the *USS Glory*. The American vessel suddenly leaned leeward, as if a violent gust had hit her sails.

The men whooped. Landon chuckled at her side. "It would seem the savvy Commodore Hall has translated the message I sent and is joining our game."

A moment later Commodore Hall hastily lowered the *Glory's* sails, again imitating the *Desire's* actions. Everyone turned their attention to the British flotilla. Sails fell in a panicked fashion, as the crews scurried to avoid what they thought was a deadly gust that had apparently caught the American ships unaware.

Her husband waited until the British masts stood stark and bare. "Now, men!" Landon shouted, ordering his courses and topsails set. "Haul all sheets to the wind! Crowd that canvas best ye can and set her loose to run free!"

Arms pumped on the lines to hoist every sail as quickly as possible. Within minutes, the *Desire* spread her wings and flew over the swells and out to sea, speeding away from the British warships.

Keelan's heart pounded furiously in her chest. It worked! Captain Hall's ship surged forward, opening the distance to the opposing frigates before they could comprehend what the American ships had done. The *Glory* even paused long enough to retrieve her long boat from the kedging.

The British, however, were not as concerned for their sailors' welfare. Rather, their long boats were cut loose and abandoned while the frigates frantically worked to hoist all available sails and quickly repair those that had been hastily cut free in a panic. Keelan laughed with glee as the *Glory* continued to increase the distance between herself and her British enemies. She turned to see Landon watching her and in her enthusiasm, smiled at him. He smiled back and her heart slammed against her ribs.

"Yer plan worked, Captain!" Gus shouted from amidships deck. "The *Glory*, she's flying! Those British devils won't catch her now!"

"Aye!" Landon agreed. "A fine plan, well executed." He tossed out a few more commands; sails were shifted, and the *Desire* turned back up the coast. He joined Gus amidships.

"Commodore Hall has helped us out many times in the past. I am honored to be in a position to reciprocate," Landon said. He glanced her way, and she caught a fleeting look of confusion. "It's time to turn our sights northeast."

An idea began to form in her mind, and she went below to seek out Daniel.

CHAPTER 7

S earch her first, indeed! No one had *ever* been able to prick her temper quicker than Landon Hart. Keelan turned the wick lower on the lantern hanging from the beam in front of the stalls, then entered and latched the door.

"I'm back, Juliet. I hope you don't mind another bunk mate." The mare nuzzled her hand as Keelan stroked her velvety nose. "I don't know what else to do. I can't bunk with the other men, and my hammock is still strung in Landon's cabin." She gazed into Juliet's gentle brown eyes. "I can't sleep with him either." The mare swished her tail and nudged the empty water bucket. Keelan sighed. "It's pretty silly, isn't it? I can't sleep with my own husband."

No doubt, if she tried to claim her hammock, he would attempt to exercise his 'husbandly duties'. She didn't think she'd have the strength to deny him again. Until he remembered her... remembered that he *loved* her... she wouldn't give herself to him no matter how badly she wanted to. As long as her love for Landon went unrequited, the act of making love by itself held no value.

IF YOU GIVE A HELLION YOUR HEART

"What if only part of his memory returns and he still has no recollection of me? What if the last five years never return? What if I never become more than an acquaintance to him?" She rested her forehead on Juliet's shoulder and closed her eyes to fight off the tears welling beneath her lids.

A soft whisper broke the silence. "Miss Keelan?"

She started at the use of her given name. The stall door creaked open and Daniel poked his head inside.

"Ahh, here you are. Ronnie and I have made a place for you to sleep in the sail closet. It will give you the privacy you require. You'll have to share space with Louis."

"Louis?" She didn't know a Louis. How would she have privacy with him there too?

"Yes. The mouser. Apparently he likes to catch a nap in there fairly often."

She gave him a grateful smile. The sail closet was much better than Juliet's stall. "Thank you, Daniel. I don't mind sharing my space with a cat, as long as he doesn't offer to share any of his catches."

❦

KEELAN AWOKE with the unsettling feeling that something was amiss. The ship barely breathed. Its usual creaks and groans, rocking and dipping were muffled, almost like when they were mired in the fog near Charleston.

The sail closet was bigger than she'd expected. It was at least as large as the master's chamber in Twin Pines, wall to wall. The actual space available was limited due to sails and equipment. Even so, Daniel somehow squeezed in a hammock for her.

She'd slept on her stomach since the lashing. The hammock enabled her to rest on her side with little discomfort. Raising up on an elbow, she found herself suddenly immobile. A shaggy orange cat snuggled against the back of her knees like a sphinx, its tail twitching near his front paws, eyes half-closed.

"You must be Louis."

The cat opened one eye, then the other, before giving her a toothy, wide-mouthed yawn. She shifted her weight, and he darted away between the rolls of canvas and out of sight.

"Thankless feline," she muttered, stumbling her way out of the sail closet.

Once on the main deck, she peered out over the flat surface of the sea with growing uncertainty. The predawn sky was purple, blue and pink, bathing everything in the low glow of dawn. Why did she still sense something wasn't right? All seemed calm and clear. No ship or storm threatened on the horizon. In fact, there was hardly any sound at all.

Perplexed, she scanned the aft deck for Landon without success, so she headed for the helm. The usual activity was suppressed. Limp and lethargic sails hung from the masts. The crew were all at ease, resting in whatever comfortable place they could find.

As she neared, the low timbre of her husband's voice drifted in conversation with one of the crewmen.

"What do you suggest?" Landon's question hung in the air for a moment.

"We could kedge her off."

"Let's do it then," Landon said.

Keelan ducked back down away from the helm and sauntered over to the rail. The still air amplified the eerie silence of the sails.

"Done with yer early mornin' duties, I hope." Gus narrowed his eyes, his voice almost booming in the stillness.

Keelan gave him a quick nod. He'd not yet forgiven her. "Good morning, Mr. Gus."

He stopped beside her and looked out over the glassy sea. "We may have to kedge off the vessel today, if we are going to make any time."

"Kedge off the vessel?" Keelan was curious as to the meaning.

"Aye," Gus nodded. "'Tis when we tie the anchor to a launch with about a mile of rope and team it with a first cutter. 'Tis then rowed out until we run out of rope. The anchor is tossed into the water. It sinks, then we weigh it back in. As we do, the weight of the anchor pulls the *Desire* to it. The anchor is raised up and tied back to the launch and we do it again."

"That sounds very time consuming," she observed.

"Aye, that it is, but 'tis better than sittin'. I imagine the captain will try to hug the coastline a bit in hopes of catching a fair breeze." He jammed his hat down on his head and rubbed the back of his neck. "As long as we stay ahead of the British lookin' ter press men like us into their navy, we'll make port in a few days."

DAY AND NIGHT, for the next day and a half, Landon's crew continued to move the ship by dropping the anchor and then heaving in the hawser, pulling the ship forward an inch at a time. It was a slow monotonous process, which frayed the nerves of even the most passive men.

Keelan helped Marcel make hard tack in the galley. She hunted for and found where most of the hens were laying their eggs and collected what she could find. She milked the goat and sneaked a small trencher into the sail closet along with a thimble-sized chunk of cheese for Louis, who always found a way to snuggle on her legs without waking her and yet shoot out of arm's reach in the morning.

At dawn on the third day a shout from the crow's nest broke the stillness, much like a dropped book in an empty room.

"Sails ahead, Captain Hart!"

All hands, not otherwise occupied, ran to the foredeck, straining their eyes to catch a glimpse of the ships mentioned.

Gus peered through the glass. "A good number of vessels ahead are stranded with no wind to fill their canvas, same as us. Circumstances are most dire for the ship in the midst of them, I would say. The one nearest to us just hoisted an American flag." He handed the glass to Landon.

Landon gave Gus a curious look before putting the glass to his eye. He moved the glass from left to right, then sucked in his breath. He didn't try to hide the worry in his tone as he answered. "Tis the *USS Glory*. I'd recognize her anywhere. She's surrounded by a fleet of four British warships."

Keelan peered at the small dark dots on the horizon and tried to make out their shapes. Commodore Hall's ship and crew simply could not be allowed to fall into the hands of the British.

"But what about the other ship? That one that just hoisted the American flag?" Gus asked.

Landon smiled grimly. "That was a trick. That ship is British, I'd bet my life on it." He handed the glass to Gus.

"How do you know?" Gus accepted the glass and put it up to his eye.

Landon gestured to the *Glory*. "Because, our friend Commodore Hall just hoisted the British Union Jack, to warn us."

It was a clever way for the American commodore to alert them of the confrontation.

"They be in no danger at the moment." Gus said, the concern in his voice betrayed the nonchalance of his words. "The ships are too far from the *Glory* to fire upon her, and the wind is too weak to move them. At this point, they be all still in the waters and can only eye each other and wait for a luff in the canvas, same as us. Shall we continue with kedging the *Desire*?"

Landon paused a beat before answering. "We could, but if the British mimic us, it could put the *Glory* in more danger."

"If we don't, Cap'n, they'll think of it soon, anyway. We might as well get a jump on 'em. We have only one anchor and hawse pipe. They may very well have two of them." Gus shoved his hands into his pockets and stared at the ships on the horizon.

Landon nodded his acquiescence. "Aye, but send a man here with flags. I have a message to send to Commodore Hall. He should be able to see from this distance."

Gus nodded and left to do Landon's bidding.

"Is there any way to help Commodore Hall?" she asked. "Can't we distract the British long enough for the *Glory* to move free of the blockade?" The commodore and Landon were friends. Surely he remembered that much. He had to help.

Landon studied her a moment as if weighing the sincerity of her question. "You know Commodore Hall?"

She shrugged. "Not personally. I was supposed to travel with him to Philadelphia, but he was called away before I could board."

Landon tilted his head and snorted. "United States Navy warships rarely take on passengers."

"It was a special favor." Her voice dropped off, and she closed her eyes, already anticipating what he would say next. Every fact she gave him sounded like a farce. Couldn't they have one conversation where her words didn't sound contrived?

Landon leaned against the rail and crossed his arms over his chest. His steely blue stare settled on her face. "A special favor for whom? I suppose you're going to tell me that I was the one who requested he take you aboard?"

She swallowed and nodded. Just once, it would be nice to have a conversation that didn't make her out to be a liar or a thief.

He leaned forward until his nose was inches from her own. "You lie."

It would have been folly to expect a different reaction from the man. She clenched her jaw tightly in an effort to prevent herself from snapping back something she'd regret later.

She failed.

Yes, she was impetuous and fiery-tempered, but he was being stubborn and nothing grated on her nerves more than trying to press sense into a thick-headed— "I'm not lying. I'll have you know, you stubborn, arrogant rake, that *you* insisted I go, while I argued to stay with *you*! Although why, is now a mystery even to me!"

He stepped forward, making her tilt her head back to glare at him, perhaps trying to scare her into recanting her words. To reinforce her resolve, she fisted her hands on her hips, and threw her shoulders back like an angry chicken. She could be just as stubborn.

She wasn't prepared for the affect his proximity had on her nerves, though. The heat from his body, coupled with the scent that was uniquely Landon's... ocean air and leather and something else... distracted her completely.

His pupils widened, darkening the blue of his irises. When he finally spoke, his voice was low and calm and so cold, it made her shiver.

"I would never put my *wife* on another man's ship. If, indeed, I *had* married again, I assure you, I would have never allowed you to stray that far, especially since I've seen the silky, soft, pale curves you hide under that leather corset."

She fought to keep her hands on her hips and her chin jutted out in defiance. She wanted to reach up and bury her fingers in the glossy, black curls that caressed his broad shoulders and kiss away the bitter, caustic tenor of his words. A warmth radiated from her palms. She looked down, shocked. When had her hands shifted to rest on his ribs? Why couldn't she keep her head around him? She retreated a hasty step back. Blast this man. She turned and fled.

His soft laugh drifted to her ears through the quiet calm. "The mice always play while the cat's away, sweet, sweet Keelan."

MARCEL INSTRUCTED Keelan to take a bucket of water to the upper deck for the crew to quench their thirst. Gus gestured her over and reached for the ladle. She surreptitiously eyed Landon from beneath the brim of her floppy hat. The sun glittered across the water and gave his skin a golden glow. He had yet to secure the ties, and his shirt gaped open, revealing the chiseled cut of his chest. She swallowed, then dipped the ladle in the bucket and served herself a drink. She filled it again for Landon when he approached.

Gus wiped his mouth with his sleeve. "What plan have ye hatched, Captain?" He raised a shaggy grey brow.

"I have an idea." Landon tucked the spyglass under his arm and drank. His gaze flickered over Keelan as he dropped the ladle in the bucket. So far, he hadn't exposed her to his first mate or any of the crew. Quite frankly, she was a bit baffled by his secrecy, especially after she'd lost her temper earlier. Perhaps he was starting to wonder if she told the truth?

"Gus, what would you do if you noticed the breath of a breeze after your ship had been still in the water for days?" Landon asked.

Gus shrugged. "I'd haul the sheets up to the wind as fast as I could."

"Aye," Landon agreed. "But what if that breeze was a stronger gust than you anticipated? What if a squall arose with such force that you worried it would flay the sails or tip the boat into the sea?"

Keelan quirked a brow. "Could that happen?" she asked, dubiously. "Could the wind really blow the boat over that quickly?"

"Oh, aye, young Mr. Mahdi." Gus nodded emphatically and rubbed his bristled cheeks. "It could indeed. And has! A gale off the coast is most unpredictable. If it catches too much sail at the wrong angle, it would tip a vessel over as easy as you could tip an empty ale bottle with your finger."

Gus moved away and began to pace while scratching his salt

and pepper beard. "If my ship be caught in the doldrums, I'd have my sails up full, to catch any puff of blow that may come my way, as we are doing." He frowned pensively. "But, if a strong wind blew in from shore and took me by surprise, I'd order the sails drawn in and furled, to avoid pitching the ship or shredding the sheets."

"Exactly!" Landon responded, eyes alight. "Any good captain conclude the same."

"I don't understand," she said. "How does that help Captain Hall and his ship?"

Landon seemed a little surprised by her question, or surprised she was interested enough to ask it. "Eventually, the stillness of the sea will be interrupted by a gust of wind, or a whisper of breeze. It can't stay like this forever. When the wind picks up, we can make it *look* as if it took us by surprise and we were actually hit by an even *greater* gust. The ship will tip; we'll haul up the sails by the brails and clew lines in apparent confusion, as if it was impossible to carry a yard of canvas."

Gus nodded and rubbed his hands together. "Then we'll drop our sheets, to make it seem we are trying to save them from being shredded by the wind!"

Landon's eyes were bright with glee. "The British ships will witness our apparent panic and they'll mimic us in anticipation of receiving the same gust." He locked eyes with Keelan and he grinned. For the thousandth time, the spell he cast with his smile made her heart jump.

"Except, we'll not fully drop our sails in said panic," Gus continued, more excited now. "But instead, allow the sheets to willow on to the deck for a few moments. As soon as the British have hastily dropped or, we hope in their panic, *cut* their sails free, we'll raise ours and catch the wind and be on our merry way before the Brits can untangle and repair their lines and haul their sheets up!"

"It will give the *Glory* the head start she needs to break free of the blockade," Landon finished with a broad smile.

It sounded like a good plan, but how would they execute it?

"How will you make it appear as if a great gust hit the ship?" She faced the shore. "What if the breeze isn't really that strong?"

"Ahhh!" Gus smiled knowingly and clapped Landon on the shoulder. "Now that is the stuff what makes this plan *brilliant*!"

CHAPTER 8

After conferring with his helmsman over the course set to Charleston, Landon turned his attention to the amidships deck where Daniel and Keelan, dressed as Kahlil and Mahdi, were about to begin a training duel. Both had their heads covered with large pieces of cloth; Daniel's a weathered white, Keelan's a faded blue. Every bit the Persians they disguised themselves to be. The crew raced up the ratlines and yard arms for a better view, as well as to give the two extra space.

Daniel had found some old planks and had created a target area, which he propped against the mizzenmast. To the target he tacked a variety of items, a rag, a chicken feather, and a strip of cloth about two feet long and two inches wide which fluttered in the breeze.

"The object of this game is to hit each of the targets on the board," Daniel said. "However, before you can toss your dagger, you must maneuver well enough away from me to make an accurate throw. You must return to the bucket before you can throw again." Daniel placed the bucket approximately fifteen feet away from the farthest target.

"That's it?" Keelan lifted her brows. "What are you not revealing?"

Good question. Landon leaned back against the railing and crossed his arms over his chest. He'd have asked the same. This should be interesting. The outcome of the earlier sparring match between Ronan and Mahdi hadn't really been a surprise. Ronan was a bigger and stronger adversary than the boy, Mahdi. But now that he knew Mahdi was Keelan, he was impressed. In all honesty, her strength and agility stunned him. Although, he had to admit, something had nagged his memory the day she'd sparred with Ronan, but he couldn't pin it down exactly. Had it been a movement? A sound? An action? Those questions kept him up that night. Even now something hovered just out of reach—a word, a breath, a vision...

His mind told him to keep the woman at arm's length, to not trust anything she said, and wait until they met up with Conal. But there was something about her that made him want to believe her. That thought dragged him back to last evening's conversation in his cabin. She could just be acting coy, perhaps expecting him to make another play before she gave in to his flirting. Somehow, that didn't seem to fit in with his observations There had been a marked transition in those deep green eyes of hers from a raw hunger to one of deep pain, when he'd offered to exercise his husbandly duties.

Daniel tilted his head sideways and shot Keelan a smug look that should make her wary. "As I mentioned earlier, you'll have to get past me."

He tossed her a training blade, a blunted saber with the tip filed flat, and gestured to her boot. "We'll use our own short blades."

Keelan gave him a sly grin. "With pleasure."

Starting in a neutral position, they circled each other. For a few seconds, they thrusted and parried, testing each other's speed and intuition, then Keelan began an earnest attack. She managed to drive Daniel back several steps before he recovered and returned in earnest.

It seemed to Landon it would only be a matter of time before Daniel would have her backed up against one of the guns. As far as a woman's skills with blades were concerned, she impressed him, but was still at a distinct disadvantage. Daniel was stronger and more experienced. She'd be no match for him. Already, Ronnie had moved closer to take her place after her defeat.

As Landon predicted, Daniel backed her up against the long gun and wedged her between the muzzle and the rail. She lunged toward him, locked her hilt with his and drove her shoulder into his chest, forcing him to stumble back a step. Before the man could recover, she had slipped over the gun and pulled out her dagger. She took a single step and threw her weapon. It struck the rag in the upper left corner. The men aloft shouted and cheered.

Daniel acknowledged her with a slight nod, but before she could make her next move, he turned and threw his blade as well. It hit the bottom corner of the rag. By the time her focus shifted from the target back to Daniel, he'd already blocked her path, sword glinting menacingly. Now the true challenge of the game became more apparent.

She circled, blocking his path to the target and preventing him from retrieving his blade. Before he could lunge, she jumped back a few steps, reached under her vest and withdrew a stiletto and sent it flying. The lower half of the chicken feather fluttered to the ground, and Landon raised his brows in surprise. Impressed, Landon laughed at Daniel's startled expression.

"You said we'd use our own short blades," Keelan tossed over her shoulder, already running to the target to retrieve her weapons. "You never said we had to use only one." She wrenched her blades free, returning both to sheaths. When she whirled to face Daniel, her eyes widened.

He stood between her and the bucket. Except now, the bucket

was twice the distance from the target. Her mouth flattened, and she narrowed her glare. "That doesn't seem very fair."

Daniel lowered his brows and smiled like a wicked pirate. "The rules have not changed. You still must be behind the bucket before you can throw your blade."

Landon perused the target. The strip of cloth Daniel had secured on the board waved almost tauntingly. He doubted there was a man aboard who could hit a moving target that small from such a distance.

Keelan cautiously approached, lifted her sword, and waved it in a serpentine pattern.

"Don't try to distract me," Daniel said. "I won't let it happen again."

She laughed and lunged. Daniel parried her attack and retaliated with one of his own, driving her farther from the bucket. She feigned left, ducked right and rolled. She sprung back in a crouch and drove her shoulder into the backs of Daniel's knees before he had time to turn around.

The man hit the deck with a thud, losing his grip on his saber, which skidded away, coming to a stop near the rail. Keelan scrambled forward like a monkey and pulled out her stiletto as she hopped behind the bucket. Daniel rolled to his side and pushed himself up to his hands and knees like an old man.

She studied the flutter of the strip of cloth. She pulled her arm back, then paused. The startling green of her eyes captured his gaze like a jewel captured a thief's. Even if Landon wanted to look at her pert, slightly upturned nose lightly sprinkled with freckles or the impish, pink mouth curved at the corners, he couldn't. Her eyes held him rooted like a wild fig tree.

She released him when she shifted her attention to the stiletto. After a slight adjustment of her wrist, she threw.

Smart woman. The men roared from the yards and Landon had to laugh at Keelan's quick mind. Rather than try to trap a moving piece of fabric, she'd instead targeted the place where it had been secured to the wood—the only part that couldn't move.

Daniel had risen to one knee, his forearm draped over his thigh. He shook his head in good-natured defeat, then stood with a smile. Keelan grinned, then turned to Landon, reached a hand to her head and gave him a jaunty salute.

As he lifted his hand to return it, she pulled the tattered blue scarf from her head, allowing her shoulder-length auburn and brown curls to fly with the wind as she mopped her face and neck before turning her attention to Daniel.

The air left Landon's lungs in a gut twisting whoosh. For a moment, he couldn't breathe. A roar echoed in his ears as if the tiger's mouth was inches away. From where it came, he didn't know, but a vision of a woman, lean and lithe, auburn hair hanging to her waist, standing in the distance... on the fringes of a pine forest invaded his mind. She had a faded blue head cloth in her hand and the edges of her mouth curled up in an impish smirk.

CHAPTER 9

Avision of the fiery-haired nymph danced through his mind and flitted away. If he hadn't already been leaning against the rail, Landon would have staggered backwards at the impact of it. A similar image had come to him days earlier, when she had sparred with Ronnie. That day, a slicing pain in his head accompanied it, forcing him to turn away and wait until it abated. The pain had diverted his attention and when he'd tried to recall the memory; it dissipated like mist swirling on a morning sea.

Today, there had been no pain to distract him, and he remembered more this time. Was it a recent memory? Could it have been a memory of Keelan? It couldn't. Could it? He tried to imagine her face without the stain.

He spun and faced the water, pounding his fist on the rail. This memory loss made him feel weak. He wasn't used to feeling weak. His men followed him because they respected his leadership. The decisions he made put coins in their pockets. They followed because they feared his temper and any repercussions that would follow a betrayal.

How could he've allowed his heart to soften again for a

woman? After what Lenita had done... nothing could have persuaded him to marry ever again. Nothing should have.

Nothing.

"Did ye see that last toss of Mahdi's stiletto, Landon?" Ronnie's voice carried a note of both admiration and amazement as he approached the helm. "I lost a weeks' share of grog to Mister Marcel on it."

Landon turned and managed a short laugh as the youth bounded up the last two steps to the helm. "I did. It was a fine throw. I doubt I could have done better."

"Marcel said she was handy in a fight, but I didn't believe him," Ronnie admitted grudgingly. "Guess I should have taken his word on it." He glanced at the helmsman's charts. "How long til Charleston?"

Landon lifted his face to the sea breeze and shrugged. "If this wind holds, before nightfall." He gestured to Ronan to follow him away from the helm and other open ears. What he had to say needed to be kept between the two of them until he knew more.

Was Keelan telling him the truth? Ronnie could hopefully clarify a few things. Between lies and truth, women lied more. They used their beauty and exotic sensuality to beguile, tame and manipulate men. This woman, Keelan, had manipulated him into a precarious position. He'd argue that his decision-making paradigm was vastly more seasoned since Lenita had betrayed him. Still... there were doubts.

Ronnie and Gus were the only others who knew of his memory loss. Ronnie, supposedly, was the only one who'd heard of his marriage. There was no one else aboard to confirm her story, except Mr. Daniel Hunter, whose word meant nothing at the moment. He was her *trusted* servant. Of course he'd lie for her. Brendan or Conal's word, he'd believe, no one else's, and it could be weeks before he'd be able to ask them.

Another thought wormed its way into his head. She could have made it all up because she'd been caught stealing the ring.

What better way to avoid the lash than telling him she was his wife?

He could have her put in irons for it. They were nearing the port of Charleston; if he didn't get his memory back before they docked, she could very well escape after playing him for a fool and stealing him blind.

He shouldn't let her out of his sight until he remembered everything. "Ronnie, you know I have no memory of your da's death nor taking Keelan to wife."

"Aye." Ronnie peered at him more closely. "Have ye started to remember, then?"

"No," he sighed. "Not much anyway." He leaned a hip against the rail. "Did you attend my wedding?"

Ronnie blinked, then shifted his weight. "Well, I was supposed to but..."

"But?"

"Well, we were waiting in Harbour Town for Conal before walking to the church when his first mate found us and told us that pirates had taken the *Seeker*." Ronan's shoulders slumped and his voice dropped, sullen and low. "Brendan weighed anchor and gave chase, leaving me behind." He kicked at a coiled rope. "I don't think he trusted me to be good enough with a saber and pistol." He crossed his arms over his chest and stared glumly over the ocean. "Then we set sail for Charleston on the *Desire*."

A jolt hammered through Landon's chest. "So, are you saying that we never made it to the church? We didn't get married?"

Ronnie shook his head, still staring at the rise and fall of the sea against the hull. "No. It had to be delayed. You told me that Keelan would have to be disguised until we left Charleston, because she had a price on her head. The crew couldn't know who she was, it had to stay a secret." He braced his arms on the rail. "I'd seen her in her wedding gown, so I already knew about her fairer sex. You didn't want me to inadvertently reveal her."

The evening he found her in his cabin, Keelan had mentioned

something about the need for her charade, but he'd been too distracted and aroused by her naked breasts to listen too much of what she'd said. It was mesmerizing, really. The dark tan line across her chest made the ivory skin almost glow in the dim light of his cabin. There was a moment when her breath had hitched, her nipples hardened into small pink pebbles, and her skin trembled beneath his fingers. That couldn't have been simply her fear at being caught stealing, could it? Desire had turned her eyes into limpid pools of emeralds. She'd been just as aroused as he.

He snapped his attention back to Ronan. This was a horrible time to relive that scene. "What kind of price was on her head?"

Ronnie shrugged a bony shoulder. "I don't know. You never gave a reason why or what the finder's reward would be." He lifted his head and stared hard at Landon. "It didn't seem to matter then."

"It matters now," Landon replied. Something swirled in his mind, becoming thicker and darker every second. What if she was looking for something else in his cabin? What if she was searching for information? Did she know he had documents for President Madison hidden in his desk? They were to go with the Freedom Runners. The British impressment of merchant crews kept increasing, and Brendan's spies had learned the British were planning attacks on New Orleans and Baltimore. After Landon read through all his journals, Gus had filled in the more sensitive information he'd dared not write down, such as the items hidden in his desk. Could he risk mentioning it to the boy? Where did Ronan's loyalties lie?

Keelan's heritage was revealed by her accent. Surely Ronan noticed. He eyed the lad. "She's British. How do we know she's not a spy? What if she had something to do with the *Glory* being called out to sea early only to be set upon by a group of British warships?"

Ronnie's eyes widened, and he glanced sideways in Keelan's

direction. "How could you possibly think that? What facts have you put together to come to that conclusion?"

Landon clenched his jaw before responding. "It's just something that's been bothering me. She told me I had arranged with Commodore Hall for her to travel north on the *Glory*; however, an American Naval vessel rarely takes passengers, especially a woman. At least not normally."

Landon rubbed his palm across his face, then gripped his head as if the pressure would fill the voids. These memory gaps were infuriating. He turned toward Ronnie. "If I had introduced them, then Hall would have considered any missive he received from her as reliable. What if she gave him false information to draw him into their trap? We have precious few warships as it is, losing the *USS Glory* would have been a devastating loss for the United States."

Ronnie inhaled deeply. "I only met her the day you were to be wed. I can't help you with anything that occurred prior to that. All I can tell you is that she's given me no reason to doubt her." He shifted his attention to Keelan and Daniel, who were now working with a few members of the crew, throwing knives at the makeshift target. "Perhaps if you make inquiries in Charleston, you'll find answers to your questions."

Landon nodded. "In the interim, keep a weathered eye on her. I've heard too many lies fall from her lips to trust her even for a second." He scowled at the chit. His gut tightened as she put her hands on her back and arched it, stretching tightened muscles. The swells and curves hidden beneath the long linen shirt and vest were imprinted on his mind from the other evening. He didn't trust her, but blast it if he didn't want her just the same.

"Well, married or not, she slept in your cabin, although the rest of the crew thinks you let her hang her hammock there because she was seasick and needed a quick path to the rail." Ronnie said.

"Damned if I remember any of it," Landon said through his teeth.

Ronnie squared his shoulders and moved his lanky frame toward the ladder. "I'm going to ask her and Kahlil to train me with long and short blades. Next time I see Brendan, I want him to regret leaving me behind like a child."

Landon stretched his shoulders, still sore and bruised. Something else bothered him. She avoided contact. Gus reached over to clap her on the back and she ducked away. Why? Kahlil— Daniel quickly stepped forward and said a few words to the first mate. The two, Keelan and Daniel, were together in whatever scheme they'd plotted. Although Daniel was old enough to be Keelan's father, he could be her partner. Maybe even her husband or… lover.

Uneasy things crawled around in his gut at that particular thought. One thing he knew for certain; both were British and not to be trusted.

He'd learn more in Charleston from his underground contacts.

CHAPTER 10

The *Desire* made port in the early evening. The sun pushed its last tendrils of light over the horizon in a final effort to grasp the day. After thanking Louis for his offering of a dead rat, Keelan helped Marcel clean up and stow away the galley staples before she went topside.

Landon had given the crew a short shore leave, but warned them the *Desire* could depart as early as noon the next day. They were instructed to keep watch for the blue Peter signal flag, which alerted the docks that the ship was preparing to leave. Landon gathered several sealed missives and left. Keelan was no longer privy to his schedule. It was hard to ignore the sinking, empty sensation that burrowed into her heart at that last thought.

Daniel had been instructed to give the horses some exercise and board them overnight at the livery near the pier, in case the captain had need for them in the morning. He'd seen to their off-loading and awaited Keelan to join him so she could spend time with Juliet, Landon's wedding gift to her.

Keelan focused on rounding her shoulders and lengthening her stride while she made her way down the plank and to the pier.

A queer dizziness had her stumbling a bit as her feet hit solid ground.

"Is something amiss?" Daniel asked, his brow creased in concern.

"How long do you suppose it takes to get one's land legs back?" She took Juliet's lead rope from him and leaned against the mare's shoulder for a moment until the dizziness faded.

Daniel chuckled, grey eyes creased with amusement. "I have no idea. Like you, I'm a lubber."

She must be getting better at acting the part of a boy. No one gave her a second look as they walked toward the livery. Still, Daniel's slate eyes shifted quickly left and right, continuously scanning the docks. Men loyal to Gampo could still be watching for her. Loyal to the pirate captain or not, the price on her head gave them plenty of motivation to keep both eyes open. Hopefully her disguise would be enough to keep her safe. Unless they knew to look for a young mulatto boy instead of a young woman with red hair.

They boarded the horses without incident, then brought Juliet and her foal into the paddock to stretch their legs. Daniel put Orion, Landon's horse, in a stall while Keelan worked with Juliet. After Daniel deemed the workout sufficient, Keelan released her from the lead and allowed the mare to wander the paddock with her foal.

She sighed, placing her arms on the corral rail. "I would give up my rations for a week to have a warm bath with soap and jasmine water." Her stomach rumbled loudly, and Daniel raised his brows. "Well, maybe not an entire week's." They laughed as Juliet's foal hopped and kicked his legs, happy to have the freedom to do so. He bounced up to Keelan and touched her knee through the fence with his velvety nose, then trotted back to pause for a moment and nurse at his mother's side.

Daniel gave her a sidelong glance. "Mrs. Schoen would probably happily prepare a bath for you in her secret pantry."

That suggestion stirred her interest greatly. "As much as I loathed being hidden away there, I'd return in a thrice for such a luxury." Could she hope for a bath? "Do you think we should risk going there?"

After Keelan had escaped from the pirates who'd kidnapped her, Daniel had hidden her at The Whistling Pig Tavern, which was also part of the Freedom Runner underground. Unfortunately, it was also favored by dockworkers and by default, spies. If one wanted to know anything happening at the docks, they only had to spend an hour or two at The Whistling Pig.

Daniel shrugged. "We'll sneak in the kitchen door." He jerked his chin toward the tavern. "We can rent a room for you and you can bathe and get a good night's rest in a bed, rather than a hammock." At Keelan's smile of delight, he laughed and added, "Come, let's get you settled, then I'll return later and put up the horses for the night."

A bath and a bed! "Thank you, Daniel." A few months ago, she'd have never placed those two things on her list of luxuries; they'd been staples—taken for granted. Amazing how quickly one's circumstances and priorities could change. Not that she'd ever choose to go back to that pampered life as a plantation owner's only daughter. She'd grown up in a British shipyard and had only lived in America a year before Landon arrived at the three-hundred acre plantation her father had purchased.

Landon. Her heart contracted in a sharp spasm. Would the old Landon ever come back to her? The thought of this version of the man remaining filled her with a dark, thick sadness. The jovial, teasing, courageous and honorable merchant captain she'd fallen in love with was not the arrogant, conceited rake he was now.

Remember me.

Charleston was a bustling port town. People were everywhere, in various conveyances, on horseback or on foot. A light cloud cover had dimmed the heat and the last of the sun's rays, making the evening walk warm, but pleasant. They cut through the marketplace where the enticing aroma of fried pies made her mouth water, and she and Daniel each purchased two of the hand-sized delights and ate both before they turned down the street toward The Whistling Pig. Familiar city sounds, like the jingle and clank of carriages and high-pitched voices of hawkers were almost as soothing for Keelan as the snap of the sails and groans of the bones of the *Desire*. She paused.

Almost as soothing?

She'd always loved the sights and sounds of city life and had never considered that a different atmosphere could ever take its place in her heart. The *Desire* provided a safe haven, and aside from recent events, had become her home. The excitement of a city bustling with every manner of humanity had been replaced by the thrill of sails snapping to catch the wind, and the exhilaration of flying over the water aboard the *Desire* with the man she loved.

A man who now thinks of me as nothing more than a cabin boy. And a thief. And a liar.

If Landon's memories were erased for good, then her path would take a completely different course. Either she would accompany Daniel north to Boston and start her life over, or stay with Landon until they met up with her brother. Conal would see her safely back to their parents, where again, she'd have to start a new life. There was no scenario that brought as much joy to her heart than the one where Landon's memories returned. She had to keep trying. Somehow she'd find a way to get him to remember that he was in love with her.

Just as they were about to duck into the alley and skirt around to the back of The Whistling Pig, Landon walked out and caught sight of Keelan. Her breath hitched. Did Mrs. Schoen say anything to him that might spark a memory? He lowered his brows and strode toward them.

"What are you doing here? I instructed Ronan to tell you to remain on the ship." He stopped in front of them, his hands clenched at his sides. Apparently nothing had changed. Wait—stay on the ship? Why?

Daniel and Keelan exchanged surprised looks. Uncertain why he would confine them to the *Desire*, and infuriated that he would even consider doing so, she stepped forward and tilted her chin up to meet his storm cloud gaze. "Ronnie had already departed when I finished helping Marcel in the galley. Daniel and I have just seen to the horses and now, if you will step aside, I'm going to enjoy a bath and a comfortable bed for a few hours."

A small muscle feathers along Landon's jaw. "You will return to the ship," he growled.

He'd not bully her. Not when the anticipation of a warm bath still swirled in her mind. "I will *not*," Keelan whispered in a hiss.

Daniel glanced up and down the thoroughfare. "Perhaps we should continue this conversation privately," Daniel said in a low voice.

Landon raked his eyes over her from head to toe, then studied Daniel, a murderous glint in his azure glare. His expression shifted to a lecherous leer. He lowered his face to hers. "No need. I think I understand your intentions."

Sounds from the street muted and Keelan's ears warmed at the harsh coarseness of Landon's words. His meaning was quite clear; he believed he'd interrupted their plans for a tryst. The skin on her face prickled as if a brush had been swept across it. She wanted to scream at him, pummel his chest with her fists until his heart hurt as much as hers, shake him until the new Landon's memories flew out, and her Landon's memories returned. It seemed at every turn, he found another reason not to trust her.

Before she could correct him, a husky female voice hailed him. "Well! If it isn't Captain Hart."

Keelan's jaw tightened at the familiar voice of Landon's ex-mistress, Annette Camsby. She glanced sideways at the open carriage, which had just paused next to them.

Distracted by the interruption, Landon did the same. His

stern countenance smoothed, and he smiled with a flash of white teeth, eyes bright with recognition. "Mrs. Wainwright, what a pleasant surprise. You look ravishing, as always." He moved to stand by the coach to offer his hand in assistance.

Annette froze. "Why, Landon Hart, I haven't gone by the name Wainwright in years. My last husband's name was Camsby, although I don't expect you to keep track." She gave a light laugh and accepted his assistance to alight from the carriage.

A flicker of frustration dimmed Landon's smile, but he recovered quickly. "My pardon, Annette," he said, using her name with the same familiarity as she'd used his. He kissed her hand and placed it in the crook of his arm. "May I offer you an escort?"

A mask of confusion fell over Annette's face as she accepted his arm and shifted her eyes back and forth between Keelan and him. When they'd last seen her, Landon had introduced Keelan to her as his wife, precipitating Annette's flight from his ship. Sensing a dissension, the woman's smile returned, and she hugged his arm to her side, just under her breast, causing Keelan's jaw to clench tighter than an angry clam.

She arched a challenging brow at Keelan, who glared back. "Of course you may escort me." Annette almost purred the words. If Keelan's gaze had been a blade, Annette Camsby would have been be slashed into a thousand pieces.

Annette adjusted her bonnet. "Were you not bound for Philadelphia? What brings you back so quickly to Charleston? Has your wife actually persuaded you to become a landlubber and run her daddy's plantation?" Annette managed to appear both innocent and beseeching.

At the word, 'wife' Landon's shoulders twitched. Yet his expression remained deceptively cool. "Plantation?" He focused his attention on Annette.

Annette's brows arched. "Why, Twin Pines, of course. The commodore left it to her when he died, or so I heard. You did know it burned down, don't you?" Annette pressed a dramatic hand to her bosom. "Most terrifying."

Keelan's stomach gave a horrified jerk. What of her aunt and uncle? Had they been there when the fire started? The Schoen's would know. When she'd left Charleston, her uncle had been about to approach Pratt, a vile man Keelan had refused to marry, about either leasing or purchasing the plantation. Something had gone wrong. Keelan clenched her jaw. "What brings you into town, Mrs. Camsby?" Or more importantly, when would she leave?

Annette waved her hand. "Oh, this and that. Mr. Pratt is having a soiree tomorrow, and I needed a new pair of gloves."

Landon returned his attention to his former mistress. Although, perhaps in his current mind, she was his *current* mistress. "It appears we have much to catch up on. Have you had supper?" He gave Annette another charming smile. His eyes conveyed a sly innuendo, to which Annette returned seductively.

"I'd be delighted," she said, giving Keelan one last smug look before smiling up at Landon. "I know the perfect place."

This was a bad dream coming to life before her eyes. Keelan shoved her hands into her pockets as far as they would go, torn between clawing Annette's eyes out and fleeing as far and as fast as her legs would take her. The fried pies churned in her stomach at the sight of Landon stepping up into the carriage. Had she lost him for good? It was obvious that Annette still wanted him. How could Landon, in the state he was in, possibly resist such a beautiful woman?

As badly as she'd wanted to pull Landon with her and Daniel into The Whistling Pig, she couldn't draw attention to them on a public street. Remaining silent nearly made her explode. Even worse, although she was his wife, she was powerless. There was nothing she could do. Never had she felt so helpless. Keelan drew a ragged breath and allowed Daniel to lead her to The Whistling Pig's rear door. It wasn't much later before the kind tavern keeper's wife had her in a small room off the kitchen with a copper tub full of tepid water. Keelan groaned out loud as she lowered herself into the bath and rested her head against the rim. Everything hurt and was either bruised, sore or sunburned. Was that peppermint? A small sachet steeped in the bath and she plucked it out and inhaled. Yes. Peppermint, Basil, and Marjoram. Perfect. She dropped it in the water and leaned her head against the rim.

Heavenly.

Mrs. Schoen poked her head into the pantry. "Here is some peppermint tea. It vill help settle der stomach." Daniel must have mentioned her earlier dizziness.

"Oh, thank you, Mrs. Schoen. I already feel much better." Not really. Nothing could upset the stomach more than interacting with Annette Camsby. She took a small sip. "It's delicious."

The stout woman beamed at the compliment. "Would madam like a few drops of der Jasmine oil in der bath?"

Her bones still ached from crashing to the deck beneath Landon, and she was sore from her last training exercise with Daniel. Camphor oil would be better. She shouldn't return to the ship smelling like flowers. But—Landon always loved the scent of Jasmine on her skin.

"Yes, please." She might regret it later, but she was desperate to dislodge his memories. Perhaps the scent of Jasmine might. He'd envelope her in his strong arms and bury his face in her neck just to inhale the scent of her skin. The sensation always made her vibrate from head to toe. A sharp yearning pulled at a spot deep in her belly. She missed him. He should be with her now, instead of with the Widow Camsby. Suddenly the small pantry became too confining. She rose and reached for the drying rag.

The image of Landon and Annette together at this same moment had her grinding her teeth to dust in her mouth, and thinking several colorful curses she'd heard aboard the *Desire*.

She had finished blotting her skin dry when Mrs. Schoen poked her head in once more. She clucked her tongue at the condition of the reopened slashes on Keelan's back. "I vill make you a salve to take. Yu must put on every day, ya?"

"I will try," Keelan replied. Her wounds had gone untended since Landon's accident, which had also apparently reopened some of them.

Mrs. Schoen shook her finger at Keelan. "No try. Do it. If your handsome man neglects dis duty, he vill answer to me."

Keelan bit her lip and nodded. She would not tell Mrs. Schoen that Landon was likely no longer *her* handsome man. He was Annette's.

CHAPTER 11

The carriage stopped before a familiar apartment off King Street. It was strange how he was constantly searching for the familiar, as if it could ground him and prevent him from flying through time, back into the blank unknown. The sense of relief at his recognition was overshadowed by a sense of incongruity. Something seemed... wrong.

Rupert opened the door and nodded a greeting. "Can I bring you anything, madam?"

Annette slid her perusal over Landon's frame. "I believe I have everything I need, Rupert. In fact, you may retire. I doubt I'll need you the rest of the evening."

Rupert had the grace to keep his expression stoic. He gave his mistress a slight bow and excused himself.

Landon followed Annette into the library, where an open bottle of Madeira awaited them. She poured herself a glass and then prepared an Irish whiskey for him. The apartment had belonged to her late husband, and the library had been designed and decorated using dark wood, leather furniture, deep gemstone colors and plush Persian rugs.

After handing him the drink, she sank to the long leather sofa and eyed him carefully. "So, you have already tired of your boyish wife? I can't say that I'm surprised, only that I hadn't expected it this soon."

He did his best to tamp down the jolt of shock that reverberated all the way into his bones. He'd offered to escort Annette with the specific intention of gleaning whatever information she might have of his current state. In all honesty, he'd not expected her to confirm his marriage at their earlier meeting; he'd been certain that Keelan had lied to him. In fact, he hadn't even considered she was truly his wife. Everything he'd observed so far had supported his suspicion that she was a spy.

Unless of course she'd been telling the truth about everything.

Hell's hounds. He wouldn't have married again. He would not have. Not *ever*. How could he even have considered it? What was it about Mahdi... *Keelan* that had completely removed every grain of common sense he'd ever had? Had he been coerced? Forced at gunpoint? Blast it all, had he compromised the girl?

There. There was a question he hadn't thought to ask.

What *were* the circumstances surrounding their vows? Had Conal demanded it? Had something else happened between him and Keelan that had forced them to marry?

But there'd been no wedding, no priest to sanctify their union. Had they even consummated their marriage? A small feminine cough reminded him where he was. Annette had asked a question of him. He swirled the amber liquid in circles around his glass. "Why would you think that I've tired of my... wife?" The word almost refused to leave his mouth. Further confirmation that marriage was not a suitable pastime for him.

She shrugged a delicate shoulder and huffed a humorless laugh. "You made it abundantly clear, when we were together last, that you no longer desired my company."

"I did?" Landon gulped a swallow of his whiskey. A question on his tongue begged to be asked. Was he ready to expose the weakness of his memory so soon? There appeared to be no other way to broach the subject other than simply asking the question. "When did you learn of my marriage?"

He caught a flicker of confusion in Annette's dark brown eyes. He shouldn't have asked in that manner. "The moment you introduced her to me as your *wife*," she said, sarcasm dripping from her words. Annette left her seat on the couch and came to him. She ran her hands up his forearms and over his chest as she studied his face. "Why are you here?"

He struggled to keep his expression one of nonchalance. Could she see the turbulent uncertainty in his eyes?

She ran a hand over his shoulder and behind his neck, then pulled his head down and kissed him. Her lips tasted like wine; the scent of roses surrounded her. Her other hand slid down over his chest.

This room was familiar. Her scent was familiar. The way she kissed him—boldly thrusting her tongue in his mouth and then nipping his lip—was familiar. By this time, he should have been lustily impatient to rid her from the hindrance of her clothes. They should both be naked on the cool leather of the couch.

Unfamiliar was the apathy he had toward the woman now. He wasn't aroused. The kiss bored him. He had a need to find a pub where he could sit alone to contemplate everything he'd learned since waking without his memories. He put his hands on her shoulders and gently broke the kiss.

She grasped his hand in hers and pulled. "Come," she whispered in a sultry voice. "Let's continue this in my bed."

Landon reached up and threaded his fingers around a strand of her sleek black hair. She closed her eyes and took a deep breath, held it for a moment, then released it.

He shook his head. "I'm sorry, Annette, I can't stay." He brushed her cheek with the back of his fingers. "But you knew I wouldn't, didn't you?"

She gave him a sad smile. "I had hoped you would." She turned her face to stare at the unlit fireplace. "But yes, the way you looked at her when you introduced us, I knew then I'd lost you." She moved away and refilled her wineglass. "I ask again, why are you here? Was it to test your resolve, or my charms? Maybe both?"

This was vexing. Why do women seem to have an uncanny ability to guess a man's intentions? "I thought I had questions to ask." He set his empty glass on a side table. But instead of answers, he had more questions.

"Do you still?"

"I think not." A small meaningless lie.

She traced the rim of her glass with her finger. "I see." She stared at him for a long moment. "Since I've dismissed Rupert, you'll have to show yourself to the door." She took a sip and gave him one last look. Sadness eased across her features and pressed her shoulders down. With a slight sigh of resignation, she left and less than a minute later, he was on the street, walking toward the wharf.

He wandered along King Street for a while, unable to return to The Whistling Pig. Instead, he entered a small pub he'd spotted down a narrow side street. He needed to form some sort of plan.

He needed to *think*.

Annette had confirmed he'd taken Keelan to wife. Twice. He was married. Even if he had wanted to ease his lust with his mistress, he would not have. He'd experienced the pain of Lenita's infidelity. Although he didn't care for this chit he'd apparently wed, he wouldn't intentionally thrust that kind of humiliation on her by committing adultery.

The dark and sparsely populated tavern suited his needs perfectly. A thick, leather-faced barkeep walked over and nodded a greeting. "What can I get you, good sir?"

Landon straddled a stool nearest the door. "An ale and two fingers of whiskey."

The man poured the whiskey first and placed it in front of

Landon, then pulled a tankard of ale. "What brings you to our fine city?" He pushed the tankard across the worn planks of the bar.

It wasn't a casual question. There were many layers of Charleston society that went beyond mere class levels. Many were underground, and Landon's response might hint his place in it. He pondered the question a moment before he answered. He needed more information about Keelan, but he'd tighten the man's lips if he asked in the wrong manner.

Honesty was always a good place to start. "I'm a simple merchant mariner," Landon said. There were a number of ships in the harbor, he'd rather not make it known he captained one of them just yet. "We made port late this afternoon and will be here only as long as it takes to deliver and pick up our cargo." He tossed down the whiskey.

The man thrust his hand across the bar. "I'm Willy Kennedy, proprietor of this fine pub."

A faint tingle along his spine sent the hair on the back of Landon's neck twitching. He grasped Willy's hand. "Ian McGill," he lied. "It's a pleasure to meet you."

Willy gestured with the whiskey bottle and Landon nodded his thanks. "What are you carrying, if you don't mind my asking?" Willy said casually, refilling the glass.

Ah. Now the tricky part. Landon smiled. "Currently, rice, indigo and several barrels of spices and port wine. We'll add items from the Lowcountry coveted by more northern ports."

Willy braced his large hands on the smooth wooden bar and tilted his head and pondered for a second before asking, "Are you familiar with Fritz Schoen? He owns The Whistling Pig."

Landon reached for his ale, aware the man's eyes keenly studied him. "Not personally, but I've heard of The Whistling Pig. Apparently his wife is a good cook."

The man nodded, glancing toward his quiet kitchen. "Aye, that she is. Wish they preferred our Lowcountry cooking. My Clara and her sister make excellent Indian corn cakes and Hoppin' John, if yer hungry."

Landon took a deep drink of his ale. "I've already eaten, but next time." A couple stout men, by their dress were likely dock workers, sat at the other end of the bar sharing a platter of meat, cheese and bannocks. The angle of their bodies suggested they'd been listening intently to the conversation.

Deciding to take a gamble, Landon leaned forward. "There was talk down at the wharf about a fire-haired woman with a steep price on her head."

The barkeep paused for the briefest second before continuing to polish the glass in his hand. The closer man of the two shifted his brusque scrutiny from Landon to Willy, who caught the man's stare and raised a brow. The dock worker gave him a slight shrug.

Landon kept his tone casual. "Do you know of whom I speak?"

Willy scratched the bristles on his cheek. "Well, yes sir, I think I might know who they were talking about. Her name is Keelan Grey, and she was last seen with a merchant captain named Landon Hart."

Landon forced a chuckle and leaned back. "So, it's true. What crime has she committed?"

A low raspy voice behind him responded, "Murder."

Landon turned his very real expression of shock to the eaves-dropping dockworker who now stood near his shoulder. Landon inched the fingers of his free hand toward a knife hidden in his boot. If there was about to be trouble, he'd be ready. "The sheriff must have a hefty reward for her capture, if she's wanted for murder." Sometimes playing a bit at being naïve made people drop their guard a little.

The tactic worked, and the dockworker snorted in derision before he answered. "Ain't the sheriff who's wanting her. It's a personal vendetta. She killed a pirate captain's first mate. He's a man whose ire you don't want to stir even the tiniest bit."

CHLOE FLOWERS

His friend added, "Word is that she's back in town. The *Desire* made port a few hours ago." He took a long swallow of his ale. "And we knows that she disguises herself by wearing britches instead of skirts."

The tar reached for a knife sheathed on his thigh. "So, which ship did ye say ye hailed from again, friend?

All eyes were on Landon, now. A sick feeling of dread seeped into his stomach.

This was trouble.

※

LANDON ENTERED The Whistling Pig and nodded to Mr. Schoen, who handed him a key.

"My wife has a message for yu," he said. "Knock on der kitchen door, she vill give it to you."

"Thank you." Landon headed for the back of the tavern. He'd managed to convince the dock workers he'd hailed from a Bostonian sloop just arrived. He bought them a round of ale and whisky, thanked them for the information and left. No doubt, the barkeep was happy for his departure.

He knocked and Mrs. Schoen gestured him into the kitchen. "We have Simon hidden upstairs," she said, wringing her apron. "Mr. Pratt somehow found out dat he vas moving runaways and tried to trap him. Tankfully, he vas warned in time to run." She let out a nervous breath. "He worries for his wife und boy."

Landon clenched his jaw. Simon had been a house slave at Twin Pines which was now, according to Annette, owned by Keelan. Interesting how *his wife* hadn't mentioned to him that she was a slave owner. What if she had partnered with Pratt? She could be trying to infiltrate Fynn's alliance, rather than spy for the British. If she was, then this mission was in even greater danger. "I'll take care of Simon's passage north," he said.

88

Mrs Schoen pressed her lips into a thin line. "He vill not go without his family."

What kind of sop had he been to marry a woman like Keelan Grey? "I'll talk to him." How had she blinded him so completely? He glanced at the stair leading to the upper floors of the tavern. If she was indeed a spy for Pratt, she was in their midst, and the one place Simon should be safe had become perilous. "Which room have you placed Keelan and her manservant?"

Mrs. Schoen's worry lines smoothed somewhat, although she still seemed confused by his question. "She iss in der last room on der right. Mr. Hunter iss in der first room."

Two separate rooms? Keeping appearances, perhaps. Landon nodded and bounded up the stairs, two at a time. He wasn't fooled. Because they each had a room didn't mean they were separated. He strode to the end of the hall and knocked sharply on the door. He heard the scraping of a chair, then the door opened a crack and Daniel Hunter's face appeared.

His gut twisted. He was right. He shoved the door wide, unable to contain his anger as he glared at the man. "What are you doing in here, have you no sense of propriety?" It took every ounce of control to keep his voice flat, and his hands at his sides. Right now, he wanted nothing more than to bury his fist in the man's face.

Hunter had the good grace to look somewhat chagrined, but remained silent. Two trenchers of half-eaten food rested on the table where Keelan sat. She lowered her fork and scowled at Landon. Without breaking her stare down with him, she said, "Please sit back down and finish your meal, Daniel." She dropped her napkin on her plate. "I'm afraid I've lost my appetite."

The dig wasn't lost on him or to his embarrassment, Hunter either.

The valet scooted to the table and picked up his plate. "I'll finish in my room, mistress."

"I'll see you in the morning." She smiled softly at the departing servant before turning her icy glare back to Landon.

Hunter gave her a quick nod and slipped out the door. Landon kicked it closed. If he managed to refrain from killing her, it might be a miracle worthy enough to persuade him to enter the seminary. Even now, green fire sparked from her eyes and the sweet smile she'd given Hunter had turned into a scowl. How many faces did she possess?

She shot to her feet, knocking her chair over. "How dare you speak to Daniel that way!" She stepped around it and approached Landon, a bundle of fiery beauty. "He practically raised me and has been nothing but a faithful servant and staunch protector. You treated him abhorrently."

Keelan stood barefoot before him, shoulders back, chin raised, dressed in breeches, shirt hanging almost to her knees. All that, along with an impish mouth, so pink and lush and kissable, awakened something in his belly that had dozed when he was with Annette. The scent of jasmine wafted into his nostrils and he stilled. A glimmer of a memory flickered before his eyes.

Wisteria blossoms drooping lazily from an arbor, an auburn-haired beauty in a gown that shown like polished silver in the moonlight. He couldn't make out her face. Was it her? Was it Keelan? He closed his eyes, desperately trying to bring it into focus, but it faded, leaving him hollow.

"Landon?" Keelan's voice was soft.

She placed a warm palm on his forearm. Opening his eyes, he stared at her. Concern creased her brow. He reached up and smoothed it, then stroked her hair, allowing a curl to curve around his finger, imagining it the color of burnished copper. He cupped her face with both hands and stared into the emerald eyes rimmed in gold.

Why couldn't he remember? He wanted to remember. He was desperate to remember. There were too many unanswered questions. There were too many treacherous situations where Keelan was involved. She'd killed someone. There was a man who would pay a hefty price for her, and one of the key people in Fynn's network had been found out. He couldn't afford a mistake.

Yet there was something else, something diaphanous and fleeting that drifted just beyond his mind's eye. Jasmine and creamy skin, russet curls and full lips. He shook his head, willing his mind to focus. Lust and common sense did not make good bedfellows. He could only move forward with the information he had now, and cling to solid facts. Not fleeting memories and the scent of Jasmine.

Fact: she was a British plantation owner.

Fact: the *USS Glory* had recently been nearly captured by a British blockade just after she'd been put in contact with her commodore.

Fact: she'd killed a man and now had a price on her head because of it.

Fact: Simon, a valuable contact within the Freedom Runner network and a house slave from the plantation she supposedly owned, had been found out.

Fact: Hunter, who spoke with a very clipped middle class British accent, was her cohort. British spy? Possibly. Even more likely, part of a vigilante group intent on wreaking havoc with the Freedom Runners on behalf of area plantation owners. He watched her face intently. There were just too many variables. Nothing made sense. "You didn't tell me you owned slaves," he finally said, each word articulated with tortured rancor. "Nor did you happen to mention that you are wanted for *murder*."

CHAPTER 12

For a moment, however brief, something in the way Landon looked at her reminded Keelan of *her* Landon. Her heart jumped at the possibility that the fog might be lifting. However, it had disappeared with the cold tone in his voice. Accusing. Angry. Wary.

"*I* don't own slaves," she replied. "Papa—Commodore Grey — did. He owned Twin Pines plantation when he was alive."

"Who owns it now?"

Where was he going with these questions? Hope surged. Perhaps he was starting to remember?

"He told me he would leave it to Uncle Jared, but my uncle said that the plantation was left to me, so I'm not certain who owns it, nor do I care." She'd left that life behind the second she set foot upon his ship.

His eyes narrowed. "And the reward for murder?"

The memory of Gampo's voice screaming her name and hurling threats at her as she ran away from the burning warehouse sent an icy trail of shivers across the back of her neck. Could their common enemy, Gampo, bring down a portion of the wall of distrust Landon had built between them?

"A man hired a couple of Gampo's men to kidnap me. I was taken to a warehouse where the pirates had stored cargo they had stolen from you." She could almost see the tension emanating from Landon's shoulders like waves of heat from a hot skillet. She held her breath and waited for him to interrupt her with exclamations of disbelief and accuse her of lying. He crossed his arms, leaned a hip against the table and waited.

She continued. "You, and my brother Conal tracked the cargo to that warehouse. You found me and rescued me from a man who'd been flaying my back with a leather strap. I later found out that man was Gampo's first mate, Crowe." A shiver skated down her spine. Crowe's thickly scarred head and yellow leer had invaded her dreams for weeks. "Gampo arrived shortly after you did. The two of you fought. During the duel, Crowe tried to stab you in the back. I used the chain that had been restraining me to pull him away from you. The fall broke his neck."

Keelan closed her eyes against the visions that surfaced as she talked. Crowe's blunt face twisted in a cruel sneer as he punished her for fighting his advances, the gleam of Gampo's saber and the wicked dagger Crowe pulled from his boot as he crept up behind Landon, chains clinking, the remnants of smoke and the metallic scent of blood. She shuddered and reached for her wine to take away the bitter taste in her mouth.

Here again, she was relating another outrageous story to Landon, who was probably completely convinced she was a habitual liar. Why would he want to believe any of this? Even though true, it still sounded outrageous. At least Gus could corroborate the part about the theft of his cargo and the fight in the warehouse. Hopefully, Landon would confirm it with him. It would be nice if he'd deem one of her stories believable.

Landon was staring at his boots to hide his expression this time, no doubt. "So Gampo has put a price on your head for killing his first."

"Apparently." Trying to explain any more might send her into a fit of hysterical laughter.

"A man was about to sink a blade into my back."

"Yes." She took a slow sip of wine and studied him over the rim of the glass. Did any of it sound familiar to him? If one tiny piece could break in to the darkness coating his memory, perhaps another might follow. Then another.

Landon unfolded his arms and began to pace the small room. His voice was low, as if he was thinking out loud rather than conversing with her. "I want to remember, because I don't understand my actions. What kind of man had I become over the last five years?" The anguish in his voice tore at her heart. "Five years ago, I would have *never* married again, let alone marry—" He gestured toward her. "Someone like you, a slaver owner and a—"

Keelan sliced the air with her hand. She lowered her voice to a whisper. "I'm *not* a murderer and I would ask that you keep your voice down. These planks are thin, and it's dangerous enough for me to be here as it is." She fought to clamp down on her temper. "Do you truly believe that I could ever be a murderer, that I could ever *intentionally* kill a person?"

He appraised her up and down, noting her petite stature and thin arms. "I've seen your skill with a blade, so I know what you're *capable* of doing."

This man! Keelan strode forward and poked him hard in the chest. "Before you make any more foolish assumptions, you should know it wasn't my intention to kill him. It was my intention to prevent him from plunging a knife into your obstinate, arrogant, thankless back!"

He grabbed her wrist and pulled her hard against him. Shock, confusion and anger rippled across his face. "I don't *recall* any of that. I don't know what to believe."

"Right now, you're believing that I'd lie to you. I want to know why." Anger made her voice tremble. She should be more patient with him, but his distrust ignited her temper faster than a match to dry tinder.

"Are you sure you want an answer to that question?" he ground out between clenched teeth. He didn't wait for her response, although he did lower his voice to a harsh whisper, "I have two theories. I'm simply not yet certain which one is correct. Perhaps you were hired to break into the inner Freedom Runner network that Fynn created."

"I knew nothing about it until the night we married," she hissed back. She pulled her wrist, but his grip didn't loosen.

His nostrils flared. "Another convenient tidbit that you cannot prove. Two, you're *British*. Perhaps you're a spy." His fingers tightened.

"You're hurting me," she snapped, twisting her wrist in his large hand. "Let me go."

He didn't release her. "It explains why Commodore Hall sailed his ship directly into an enemy flotilla."

He reached his other hand up to grip the hair at her nape. He tilted her head back and stared into her eyes. "Perhaps both theories are correct. Tell me, *wife*, did you spread your legs for him, too?"

Keelan's other hand flew up and slapped his face with a sharp, painful crack even before her brain registered the movement. "How dare you?" The blood drained from her face so fast it left her dizzy; her hand throbbed and her palm burned. The heat from Landon's body pulsed into the center of hers, his scent filled her nostrils and the irises of his eyes virtually crackled with a livid azure fire. His breath hitched and for a second, his breathing stilled, his mouth slightly open.

He started to say something, but the next second his lips were on hers. The sensation from the contact sent a quake through her body; her heart rumbled and blood roared through her veins. His mouth moved against hers, unyielding and relentless. Her fists clenched his shirt; the skin tightened across her knuckles and her nails bit into her palms through the fabric. The familiar taste of his lips and the light stubble on his chin had her melting. His tongue possessed her mouth, searching, demanding, punishing.

She wanted him.

Dear Lord, she wanted him.

She unclenched her fists and dove her fingers into his sleek black curls and kissed him back with all the fear, frustration and anger she'd held inside since the night she'd disappeared from his memories.

Remember me. Remember us.

Her hands sought his warm velvet skin, sliding under his shirt and bumping over the hard ridges of his ribs. He groaned in her mouth, the vibration radiating through her core.

Landon released her hair, but only to tear her shirt open. Then his hands were on her chest and he pushed her back against the wall, pressing the length of his hard frame against her. His hands were wreaking havoc on her bare skin. He kissed the air from her lungs. Their kiss created a fire cloud low in her belly, melting some things, incinerating others.

The old Landon had made love to her reverently. Slow and passionate, he had worshipped her body. Heated caresses and velvet words. But this was a different Landon. This Landon was fueled by anger, frustration and betrayal. It was both frightening and exhilarating. She reveled in the heat of his skin, like warmed marble. He had never kissed her with such passion and fury. His words still stung, and she poured her hurt and pain and longing into the kiss.

She wanted him, good Lord, how she wanted him, but not like this. If he carried her to the bed, she would be helpless to resist. That thought triggered the memory of his chest and stomach pressed against hers. Skin to skin. His exhale, her inhale. Sleek, hot, heady with passion.

If she allowed him to tumble her in bed, she'd reinforce his earlier insinuation, which still pierced her heart like a thin stiletto. She wanted him, yes—but not this way, not saturated with anger, and radiating jealousy and lust. This—it ignited her desire, yes, but something was missing, out of balance.

There was no connection. Her love for him had nothing to grasp. It couldn't meld with the emotions emanating from *this* Landon.

Because those emotions didn't include love.

It was that thought, which cleared her mind from the heady delirium of his kiss, his touch. She tore her mouth from his and shoved him, twisting away. "Stop, Landon." He reached for her and she slid behind the small table, putting it between them.

He stood clenching his jaw, eyes closed. Ragged breaths betrayed the calmer demeanor he attempted to show. She clutched the edges of her shirt together, hating what she had to say next.

"I love you, Landon, but I can't... not... like this. Not... Please leave." The words festered like acid in her mouth. If she said anymore or tried to explain further, her resolve would crumble. If she allowed him to argue with her, her resolve would crumble. Hell, if he even opened his eyes and looked at her, she would pull him into her bed and she would become the woman this Landon believed her to be in his fragmented mind.

In the morning, he would despise her even more.

CHAPTER 13

Keelan tossed in her bed like a dingy on a stormy sea. Even the quiet that followed after the tavern closed didn't invite sleep. She'd shed her breeches, choosing to sleep in the shirt Landon had given her the last time she'd stayed at The Whistling Pig. The air was still hot and humid. Even the open window didn't lure the slightest breath of a breeze. It wasn't the heat, however, keeping sleep at bay.

There was one single moment in time that would not rest in her mind. Before he left, Landon had paused with his hand on the knob and studied her. She'd stood in the center of the small room, her hands clenching the linen shirt over her heart. His eyes fastened on her face and his brows drew a tiny bit closer in consternation, as if the truth was written on her skin.

Remember me.

In the back of her mind she had been hoping with all her heart that the moment she kissed him back, his memory of her would return. In fact, she had hoped it so hard that she believed it to the point of almost expecting it to return the moment their lips touched. But the hard planes of his face hadn't shifted from wary distrust to recognition and love as it had in her daydreams.

The moment came and went, then Landon wordlessly stepped into the hall, then closed the door.

She flopped to her stomach and buried her head in her arms. Without Landon, she was frayed and shredded like a broken rope that had snapped from the tension of too heavy a burden.

A small click interrupted her meanderings. She turned her attention to the doorknob. Hope flared, followed by uncertainty. If it was Landon, would she be able to turn him away? Should she? Perhaps his memory had returned. A moment of quiet followed, then a small scrape invaded the silence.

Another scrape. This time the sound came from behind her.

She snapped her attention to the open window, now blocked by a shape that was too narrow in the shoulders and too short to be her husband. Icy fingers of fear gripped her spine, and she reached for the knife hidden under her pillow. The figure lunged toward the bed and Keelan screamed, rolling backward off the other side. She scrambled to her feet and lashed out with her blade, forcing her attacker to jump back. He circled the bed and lunged, slashing through the fabric of her shirt and across her ribcage, causing her to arch back involuntarily at the sting. Her foot snagged the blanket, and she fell.

He tossed her a malicious grin. "I have ye now, missy. Ye killed me brother and now I'm returning the service. A life fer a life."

Her voice came out thin and raspy. "Gampo?"

He chuckled. "Nay, but I used his name in order to loosen a few tongues."

Throwing a blade while on her back was both awkward and unreliable, but she had no other choice, especially since he could throw his at any moment. Since he was after revenge, chances were he'd want a closer, more intimate kill.

That decision was going to cost him.

Keelan rolled to the left, adjusting her grip before letting it fly. He ducked and dodged, but not fast enough. The knife missed its mark and bounced off his rib. That would likely not even slow him down. She was at a fatal disadvantage now. The dark shadow stalked her, the knife twitching in his hand. She cast a frantic look around for another weapon.

A loud crash froze both of them as Daniel stumbled in, sword in one hand, dirk in the other. Keelan scrambled to her hands and knees and lurched toward her knife. The assassin flipped the dirk in his hand, drew his arm back and threw the knife at her.

The world seemed to slow in that moment. There was no way she could out maneuver a flying dagger at such close range. If his throw was true, she'd likely be dead before her next heartbeat. A strangled scream broke from her throat, then Daniel flung himself across her body.

There was no mistaking the sound of the blade sinking into his back.

"No!" she screamed as Daniel's momentum sent him sprawling past her. The murderer bolted to the window; his movement making Keelan instinctively grab the dagger from Daniel's back, twist and throw it. The blade sank into the man's neck with all the rage and despair that exploded from her heart like an ignited powder keg. A guttural noise escaped from his throat before he fell to the alley below.

Sobbing, Keelan dropped to her knees and reached for Daniel, praying that the blade missed his heart. A long, hard arm snaked around her waist and pulled her to her feet, and a hand covered her mouth before she had time to scream again.

Landon's voice rasped low and firm in her ear. "Stop struggling, Keelan, it's me." He turned her toward him and held her tightly. For a moment, she allowed herself the luxury of relaxing in his arms, inhaling the calm authority that emanated from him. She couldn't help Daniel if she allowed herself to panic. But her friend was not moving.

A horrifying, stoney fist gripped her heart and squeezed. Her stomach took a sickening dive. "Daniel—"

"I'm sorry, Keelan," Landon murmured into her hair. "Nothing can be done for him now." He turned toward the door where Simon stood waiting. "Get her out of here, Simon. You know which passage to take. Go."

Simon grasped her wrist, but she pulled away from him. They had to take Daniel first. They had to help him. "No! Daniel's hurt! Let me go!"

Landon took her face in his hands. "We can't help him, Keelan."

She shook her head frantically. He can't be dead. Not Daniel. She spun toward the man who'd practically raised her, and a wretched sob burst from her throat at the sight of his back drenched with blood. A tremendous weight descended upon her shoulders and the floor gave way beneath her.

Landon grabbed her and swept her off her feet, then dumped her in Simon's arms. "Get her out of here!"

"I'm sorry, Miss Keelan," Simon said earnestly. Before she could reply, Simon hefted her over his shoulder. She could barely take a breath, let alone vocalize her outrage as he took her from the room.

Doors opened and panicked voices drifted up from the second floor. A dim light illuminated the stairwell. Simon strode to the far end of the hall and opened a small closet. Placing Keelan on her feet, he gently pushed her inside and reached past her to release a latch on the back wall. A narrow door swung open. He gripped her elbow then closed the hall door, plunging them in total darkness.

The small space filled with her heaving sobs. Simon squeezed her elbow. "Sorry, Miss Keelan, but I'll have to lead you. The steps are steep, but I know 'em well and can guide you down." Simon must have understood that shock and grief had frozen her tongue; he didn't wait for her to answer and instead quietly pulled her down the steps.

The best she could figure was that they were descending a stair inside the rear wall of the tavern. Beyond the hidden staircase was a low, narrow passageway. It smelled of dirt and onions, and the air was stale and hot. It wasn't long before rivulets of sweat ran down the side of her face and between her shoulder blades. Simon groped his way along the wall and a few minutes later, he stopped. A soft click echoed in the dark and a rush of fresh air enveloped Keelan. She took a deep breath.

Simon released her arm. "Stay here while I check da street. You follow when you hear my whistle. Close the door soft and it'll latch well enough." He slipped out silently.

Keelan glanced down the passageway which opened up to a narrow walk between two buildings. Simon's bulk filled the space as he shuffled sideways toward an alley. He paused at the end. A few seconds later, she heard a soft whistle.

She'd only taken two steps before she heard a shout. Then another.

"Hold!" A pause. "Hey, I recognize this negro!"

"Mac! Look who we found!" another voice yelled.

There were sounds of a scuffle, muffled grunts and expletives. She scooted back to the door and tried to pull it open, but it wouldn't budge. Unable to fetch Landon, a new surge of fear rushed over her; she was still clad in only her long linen shirt. She had no weapon. No way to help Simon. Praying the buildings blocked the moonlight enough to veil her in darkness, she sank to her belly and crawled toward them. At least she could try to get a glimpse of their features, or perhaps even identify them.

"Ho, lads! What's going on here?" Landon's slight Irish lilt drifted down the alley, and she sagged in relief.

"We've caught a runaway, is all."

"How do you know he's a runaway?" Landon asked.

"Been looking' fer 'im near two days now. We work fer his new master."

The sound of clanking chains was followed by a pained grunt. "Dammit, Mac. Why'd'you do that? Now we gotta carry him and he ain't gonna be no light load."

"It's a good thing there's four of you," Landon said dryly.

A harsh laugh. "I think Brewster's nose is broke. Coulda used two more. Mister Pratt has plans to make an example outta 'im. This one can expect a long fall from a short rope by sunset tomorrow, that's fer sure."

Landon's tone seemed casual, as if he was discussing the weather or last night's supper, but Keelen's ears picked up the steel behind it. "Since you have everything in hand, I'll return to my room. There's been a lot of excitement tonight. Some sorry cur fell from the third-story window earlier."

"You don't say," one of them muttered. "Well, you can go get back to bed now. We won't be disturbing the quiet of yer slumbers no more."

She heard the grunts of the men as they moved their burden away as well as Landon's steps in the other direction. Now she was in a quandary. Follow Simon's captors or wait for Landon to find her. The rest of her clothes were back in her room at the tavern. She stayed still for a few moments, contemplating.

"Keelan?" Landon's whisper was barely audible. He'd returned to the end of the narrow walkway near the alley and slipped in.

"I'm here," she whispered back.

"I have your things, we have to go. The tavern is already roused, and the Schoen's will have to send for the sheriff soon."

She scrambled to her feet as he approached. He handed her a bundle. It was her breeches and boots, thank goodness. She dressed in jerky movements, vaguely aware that tears were streaming down her cheeks.

Dear dear Daniel. He'd been with her for her entire life. He'd sacrificed his life for hers, something she certainly didn't deserve.

"Today, you're going to learn how to ride astride a horse," Daniel had told her when she was seven.

She stood in boy's breeches and boots, thrilled at the prospect of learning how to ride, but feeling tiny next to the bay mare.

"You may never have a need for this skill, but should the occasion ever arise, it's crucial that you accomplish it well."

When she turned ten, Daniel handed her a short blunted sword. "This is a rapier. It's an elegant weapon we shall use to introduce you to the necessary footwork you'll need to learn in order to better master the craft of fencing."

"I'd rather ride my pony."

"Then why aren't you?"

Embarrassment and indignation heated her cheeks. Minutes earlier, she'd gotten into a tussle with one of the stable boys, who'd pushed her to the ground and skinned her elbows. Daniel had just finished wiping away the blood. That mean boy would never catch her if she was fleeing across the heath on her pony, but she couldn't get to her pony if he wouldn't let her in the barn.

"Should you ever find yourself in another unfortunate situation, would you like to have the ability to defend yourself?" he'd asked in a casual tone.

That got her attention. She soon became an avid student, and it wasn't long before the stable boy quit trying to bully her away from the barn.

Daniel, once Papa's valet and her tutor, had settled in her heart like a treasured family member.

Now he was gone. A thorny guilt scraped her chest along with the knowledge that she was the reason Daniel was dead. She should have grappled for better balance before throwing her dirk. She'd been too hasty, too rattled for an accurate throw.

Pausing long enough to wipe her eyes with her sleeve, in the corner of her eye she caught a second figure beside Landon. Ronnie nodded a solemn greeting and fell in step behind her while she did her best to mimic Landon's catlike stealth as he led the way.

Landon headed toward the *Desire* with slow deliberation and care, pausing frequently to search the night for other figures following or hiding in shadow. They halted across the thoroughfare from the pier. Inky swells slapped the pilings in time with the creaks and yawns of the sleepy vessels anchored nearby. Although there was no movement, Landon's stillness kept her frozen. She tried to peer more closely into the darkness. He touched her shoulder, then with his finger on her chin directed her attention to a stack of crates. It took a moment for her to pick out the irregular shadows in the moonlight. Two men were taking turns keeping watch, one slept, the other scanned the ship and the wharf.

This was puzzling. The pirate who'd used Gampo's name to put a price on her head had used whatever information he'd been given to find and attack her. So whose men were these, and who were they watching?

When she voiced that question, neither Ronnie nor Landon had an answer. They backed into the shadows and retreated. They'd need extra hands if they were going to go after Simon. They trudged in silence to the livery, the quiet of the dark broken only by an occasional night creature shuffling in the shadows. A bleary-eyed groom answered Landon's knocks and allowed them in after examining his receipt. The boy gratefully headed back to his bunk when his assistance was waved away. The three didn't speak as they saddled Orion and Juliet. The foal whinnied when they led the horses from the livery, prompting Juliet to return a low whicker.

"Hush, Juliet," Keelan murmured. She patted the sleek, gray neck to reassure the mare. "We'll return for your baby, don't worry."

They stayed off the main streets and meandered their way out of town. After they left the city of Charleston, Landon finally spoke. "We're going to a safe house. It's on the border of Twin Pines..." He shot a glance at Keelan. "And Oak Leaf."

Oak Leaf was old man Pratt's plantation. That wicked man who'd tried to barter for her hand in marriage a few months ago. She shuddered. Too many stories floated around about how heavy-handed he was with his female slaves. Uncle Jared had waved them away, but Daniel had always said that in the fabric of every rumor, a thread of truth is woven.

Now, Simon was there, awaiting his doom. "We can't leave Simon behind to be hanged," she said.

Landon's jaw clenched. "We won't," he replied.

Ronnie turned back to look at her from his place behind Landon's saddle. "We'd been discussing a plan to get him to the ship when you screamed."

His words brought forth the vision of Daniel, crumpled on the floor, still in death. Fresh tears burned her eyes as the thick, dark arms of grief wrapped around her chest. The horrible guilt that assailed her made it even harder to breathe. Had Simon not needed to take her from her room, he wouldn't have been caught. It was a moment before she realized they'd stopped and she was choking on sobs.

Without saying a word, Landon pulled her from Juliet's back. He murmured low resonant words and his chest rumbled while he spoke, but she was too distraught to make out what he said. He stroked her hair. He held her there, on the side of the road, until her tears were spent.

Finally, she turned away from him and wiped her face with her sleeve. Landon touched her shoulder, but she didn't want to look at him, especially now with her nose red and her eyes swollen. Yes, she was being proud about her appearance at a time it was useless to do so, but he already despised her. Why compound it? Her shoulders sagged. In truth, she didn't have the strength to care what Landon thought at the moment.

An ironic smile twisted her mouth. She was dressed in boy's breeches, boots and a dirty, frayed, blood-stained shirt. Her hair was a startled, wild spray of curls scared out of bed by an assassin, then exposed to the hot humid air of a South Carolina summer night. She couldn't look any worse of a fright, anyway.

"Keelan, you have my sincerest condolences," Landon whispered.

She could only nod.

"I'll find a way to have him properly buried, perhaps near Commodore Grey," he added.

Her voice was soft and reedy. "That would be nice, thank you."

He touched her shoulder again. "I want to take you to a safer place. Can you ride?"

In answer, she turned and remounted Juliet and adjusted the reins. She was grieving, not incapacitated. He nodded his approval, then mounted Orion. There was an edge of pity in Ronnie's eyes. She tried to reassure him with a small smile.

Keelan recognized their surroundings now. In the dim light of the predawn, the dilapidated cabins hunched in the dewy meadow like arthritic old men. One had completely collapsed, the others had partial roofs and walls. She and Landon had taken refuge here during a horrible tempest a few weeks ago. Her face flushed at the recollection of the kisses they'd shared. She'd lost her heart to Landon Hart that day.

Certainly unaware of the places Keelan's thoughts had meandered, Landon had stopped in shock, taking in the collapsed cabins and general destruction of the area.

She grimaced. Yet another memory they no longer shared. "A hurricane hit the Lowcountry a few weeks ago," she explained. Ignoring her, Landon dismounted and walked through the debris toward a crumbled chimney. He wouldn't find what he was looking for. The trap door next to the chimney was now covered by crumbled bricks. "It's blocked," she said. "The chimney collapsed on it during the storm."

He stopped and whirled back to stare at her. "How did you learn about this place? It's been a secret refuge for years."

Keelan dismounted, pondering how to answer him without giving him another story he'd call ludicrous. She heaved a sigh. No matter what she said, he'd only believe half of it. "Because you and I were hiding in the cellar when the chimney fell." She walked to the tunnel entrance behind a large boulder a short way from the shanty. "It's probably an even better hiding place now, than before the storm."

His face remained impassive. "But how did you learn of the hidden cellar?"

Here it was. She'd turn around and look at him and he'd be glowering at her, distrust in his narrowed eyes and firmly set mouth. It was a wonderfully kissable mouth that had done very talented things to her in the near past, but now only irritated her. "I know because you brought me here to seek shelter from the hurricane."

His expression, rather than accusatory or wary, seemed more pensive this time. Did she dare hope that he was starting to believe her? Landon walked over to the hidden door. "Ronnie, stay here with Keelan. I'll send word when it's safe for you both to return to the *Desire*." He pulled the pile of dead branches away from the opening. "You should expect to be joined by Simon's wife and son. They are to attempt an escape tonight during Pratt's party. Gus and I will get Simon out."

Ronnie's expression darkened. "Why can't I come with you? I don't want to hide with the women and children."

Landon gave Ronnie a stony stare. "Because it will be easier and less noticeable with just Simon and me, and I need someone I can trust to stay here." He gathered Juliet's reins from Keelan.

Ronnie's eyes flicked to Keelan and back to her husband. Landon's words hit her like a punch to the stomach. She shut her mouth with a click of teeth, unaware it had dropped open. "You *still* think I'm a spy?" Her voice rose in pitch. "You honestly think I would give up Simon's family? That I would turn Ruth and Joseph over to that... that *monster*, Pratt?"

Landon held up his hands, his face smoothing into those cool lines and planes. "Keelan—"

Enough of this! What more did she need to do to prove herself to this stubborn, insensitive, and downright *obstinate* man? Anger flared in her chest, fighting for space with the grief that had already settled there. She wanted to hit something. If Landon's jaw wasn't as hard as his head, she'd start there. It was possible she was being slightly unreasonable and probably over-reacting to the situation, given Landon's current condition. His memory loss was frightening, but for her, his distrust was tragic.

She snatched Ronnie's dagger from his waist and before either of them moved, she grabbed one of Landon's raised hands and slapped the grip into his palm, then pulled the blade to her chest. When Landon drew it back, she stepped into it again. "If you don't trust me, then kill me now." Her voice shook, although she wasn't sure if it was from anger or her fragile grip on her emotions.

Since the day he lost his memory her heart had been continuously nicked by Landon's contempt, like a rapier flicked flesh off the bone one tiny piece at a time. "Every day you don't remember me, every time you doubt me or look at me with displeasure, scorn or distrust cuts into my heart and slices off a piece. I can no longer stand the pain, Landon. End it."

His eyes widened in shock. She moved the blade from her heart to her throat and pressed it into her flesh, locking her gaze to his. "Or simply slice my throat if it's easier. No one will know but you and Ronnie. Daniel is... gone," she barely choked out the word. "Conal is not here to tell you that you're being a fool. Our cousin Brendan is not here to confirm it. There is no one to miss me and ask questions, at least not right now." She pressed the blade harder against her neck. The sting of the steel breaking her skin came nowhere close to the cold metallic ache of despair shattering her heart.

CHAPTER 14

With a stifled curse, Landon pulled the blade away from Keelan's neck and tossed it to the ground. He reached up and gently brushed the blood away, then traced a finger along her jaw before he cupped it in both hands. He stared for a long moment into her eyes, his own darkening from a cold crystal to a deep indigo. His pupils flickered and widened, then he lowered his head and gently pressed his mouth to hers.

She closed her eyes and focused on the warm softness of his lips, the brisk stubble on his chin. Her mouth clung to his for a moment before he pulled back and searched her face. "I feel like I should know you," he whispered hoarsely. "Your eyes are familiar to me. I see fleeting glimpses of images, sometimes in my dreams, sometimes when I watch you. It's like holding water in my bare hands. No matter how hard I try to retain it, it still seeps away."

"Stop trying," she said, pulling his head down again to rest his forehead against hers as if she could press her memories into his mind. "Just open your heart enough to trust me, everything else will come to you in time."

He tilted his head. What was he thinking? Emotions were churning inside, certainly. Confusion? Yes. Frustration? Of course.

Bewilderment? That was interesting and good. It meant he wasn't fighting reality; he was thinking about it, analyzing it.

Instinctively, she pulled his face closer and kissed him. Lips were soft, pliant, gentle. His mouth moved slowly, almost tenderly over hers before he took the tip of his tongue and stroked her lips open. Eyes closed in bliss, Keelan prayed for time to cease long enough for her to catalogue each touch, each sensation of this kiss into her memory. She wanted to remember his scent, the warmth of his lips, the moist heat of his mouth. If he never recalled their past, then she would create a new memory with him now, in the present, one they would both have in common from this moment forward. If they never kissed again, at least she'd burn this one kiss into her heart and mind.

So, into this kiss, she poured her love, devotion and faith. Their tongues and lips stroked and moved in a slow, deep, sensual dance and time did stop. The clouds paused in their drifting; the earth paused in its spinning. It was as if the entire universe was waiting to exhale.

Landon broke the kiss, pulled her closer and enveloped her in a tight hug. He rested his chin on the top of her head and inhaled. "Jasmine," he murmured.

Ronnie's cough interrupted them. "I got the door open and the lantern lit in the cellar."

LANDON MADE sure they were settled comfortably before he left with both horses. It was only then that Keelan twisted and evaluated the wound on her side. She waved Ronnie away when he offered to help. The slashed shirt wasn't too bloody around the opening, a good sign. She dampened a cloth with vinegar from the stores left in the cellar. She washed the wound, sucking air through her teeth as she worked. Once she had it cleaned, she found a bag of rags and wrapped it. Nothing left to do but wait for Ruth and Joseph to arrive.

Since their sleep had been cut short the night before, she and Ronnie alternated napping and keeping watch. He'd insisted that she sleep first, and when she awoke and peeked outside, the sun was at its zenith. She took care of necessities and when she returned, she was glad to find Ronnie had stuffed the bag of rags she'd used earlier under his head and now slept soundly.

To pass the time, Keelan wandered around the cellar and took inventory of the supplies stashed there. Baskets of root vegetables, tattered blankets, jugs of whiskey-laced water, and of course the vinegar she'd used on her cut. She noticed a pile of clothes. Perhaps there was a shirt in better shape than the one she had on. She sifted through the clothing, and found a skirt and blouse, which she could exchange for her britches and tattered shirt. There was also a large tin of hard tack on the shelf, which she returned with a defined shudder. She wasn't hungry enough to munch on *that* yet. In fact, just the smell made her nauseous; she'd have to be close to starving before she'd even lift the lid again.

The sound of a loud snort drew her to the tunnel. She lowered the lantern wick and stepped toward the exit.

A child called out softly, "Hulloo. Anyone here? Capt'n Hart?"

Recognizing the voice, Keelan went outside. Joseph, Simon's son, sat on Old Poke, the mule her uncle had kept as a companion to his brood mares. The child was alone, which was unnerving. "Hi Joseph. Where's you mum?"

Joseph stared at her long and hard for a moment before recognition flooded his features. "Miss Keelan! Dat really *you*?"

She laughed. "It is, I'm afraid," she said, glancing down at her attire. "I know I've looked better."

"Well, you still a sight for sore eyes, my mama would say." He slid off the mule's back and reached up for his crutch. Joseph had been born lame. At Twin Pines, he did tasks that didn't require much speed or movement, like tending the smokehouse and the chickens.

She became more concerned by his mother's absence. "Why isn't your mum with you, Joseph?"

Joseph bit his lip, but his eyes still welled with unshed tears. He swallowed a couple of times before he choked out his words. "Mastah Pratt locked her in the shed with daddy. He told dem to put me in too, but I hid. Thomas left Old Poke in the paddock and so I rode him here to get Mister Hart."

Keelan couldn't stop her gasp of shock. "Joseph, taking Old Poke, was dangerous! What if you were caught and charged with horse thieving?" she said. It was likely he would've never been actually charged with a crime. Pratt would have had his men hang the boy on the spot.

"Before I left, I crawled up to the back of the shed to talk to mama and daddy. Dey told me to come right here and warn you and Capt'n Hart."

"Warn us about what?" The hair on the back of her neck tingled.

"Mastah Pratt know all about Capt'n Hart smugglin' runaways on his boat. He planning to send men to search it tonight. Dat why he invited Capt'n Hart to his party this evening. Mama heard Pratt say he'd 'smite him with the hammer of justice'." Joseph peered into the tunnel. "You need to tell him not to go to the Mastah Pratt's party, tonight Miss Keelan. He gots to leave Charleston soon as he can. Mastah Pratt plan on killin' him."

Keelan grabbed the rope attached to Old Poke's halter. She had to ride and find Landon. The distance from the sun to the horizon told her that was late afternoon. If Landon intended to attend the party, he'd bathe and dress in his cabin on the ship. Chances were that he was still there. She tied Poke's rope to a bush. "Follow me, Joseph. We need to get you settled so Ronnie and I can go warn Captain Hart."

THE RIDE back to Charleston on Ole Poke was bumpy and painful for all involved. Keelan and Ronnie both shared space on the mule's bony back. His gait matched the terrain and after the second mile, it was impossible to tell if it was the lumpy, rutted road or the mule's gait that jolted them up, down and all directions in between. The soreness would likely last for days.

Both Ronnie and Keelan expelled a relieved breath when they finally trotted up to the livery stable. A groom stepped from the barn to take Ole Poke's bridle and looked at the two of them with suspicion. "Good evening. Will you be boarding your... er... mount for the night?"

Keelan nudged Ronnie, who snapped to attention and answered. "Uh... no. No, thank you," Ronnie said. "Captain Hart sent us. We only need to leave Ole Poke here for a short time."

The groom huffed out a visible sigh of relief. "I'm familiar with Captain Hart. I'll take care of your mount." He left with the mule and Keelan and Ronnie walked briskly to the *Desire*.

Hopefully they weren't too late.

ELLE AND YANDA sat on the floor in the galley, mending one of the smaller sails damaged during the storm. Marcel knew the slaves hid in the false wall in the forward hold, because he was the one who let them in and out of the hiding place. The cook folded his arms across his bony chest. "Non, he is not here. Gus and ze capitan left just before the last watch changed." He shifted his attention to the runaways and jerked his chin in the direction of the secret cargo hold. "You all must hide." They wordlessly jumped to their feet and slipped from the galley.

Keelan and Ronnie exchanged glances. Now what? Without

Gus, she had no one else to ask for help. She'd known Marcel only a short time. Could she trust him?

Ronnie squared his shoulders and stepped forward, surprising Keelan. Without his older brother around to eclipse his shadow, Ronan now straightened his back in confidence. "Captain Hart is in danger, and we need to gather the men to help him."

"Where is he?" Marcel narrowed his eyes. "And how do you know he is in danger?"

Ronnie looked at her and she nodded. They had no choice. If Marcel was truly loyal to his captain, he would help them. "Simon has been captured, and the captain went to Pratt's to break him free." Ronnie said.

Marcel's shoulders tensed. "*Oui*. He insisted only Gus accompany him."

"He's walking into a trap," she said. "Pratt knows he's been helping runaways."

"Who are you to know these things?" Marcel demanded. Although his voice had roughened, his face had paled.

Ronnie shifted his weight. "Mister Marcel... umm... Mahdi isn't really... Mahdi."

The cook's eyebrows slammed down. His stoney glare switched from Ronnie to Keelan. "What eez this nonsense?" he demanded.

There was no going back now. They had to trust Marcel. "What he means to say, is that I'm not Persian, nor am I a boy," she said, keeping her voice calm. The last thing they wanted was for Marcel to explode and cause a commotion.

He pointed at her. "Zat, I knew." He lifted a shoulder. "Or at least I suspected."

Now she was wondering who else suspected. Adopting male mannerisms was no easy task for a female. Although, perhaps the opposite was also true.

Ronnie lowered his voice to a whisper. "There's more, Marcel.

She's Captain Hart's *wife*," Ronnie said, stepping back, a look of uncertainty clouding his face.

Marcel sputtered for a moment, looking back and forth at the two as if expecting them to tell him they were having fun at his expense. When they didn't, he threw his hands up and released several strings of French profanities while retrieving weapons and strapping a gun belt around his waist.

Keelan expelled a long sigh of relief. She hadn't realized she'd been holding her breath. "You must gather as many men as you can, rent a wagon from the livery and go to Pratt's plantation to help the captain," Keelan said.

Marcel nodded, his face grim. "I will get zee men. *You* two," He wagged a finger between the two of them. "Will stay on zee ship." Muttering under his breath in French, he hastily departed.

Ronnie and Keelan exchanged defiant stares. They, of course, waited until he left the galley. She wasn't about to stay behind, and from the look on Ronan's face, neither was he. She pulled out the old servant's skirt she found in the cellar. "I have an idea, follow me."

🝖

KEELAN TOSSED a shift on the bed.

"Why me?" Ronnie whined.

Keelan took a slow, patient breath. She needed Ronnie's full cooperation. If either of them showed any hesitation, wariness or fear, they'd be caught. "I would draw too much attention and run the risk of being recognized. I'll pass scrutiny better as a servant," she said, pulling more clothes from the trunk in Landon's cabin. "We can't wait until Marcel and the men are ready to depart. We must leave now. We'll rent a carriage from the livery."

Grumbling, Ronnie shrugged out of his shirt. "This had better work."

CHAPTER 15

Landon tried again to focus his attention on Annette. She'd talked incessantly since he'd helped her into the carriage. Her posture told him she believed he'd changed his mind about continuing their relationship. Since it suited his plan, he said nothing to dissuade her from that assumption. She'd not guess until much later that he'd used her for an easy entry to Pratt's property. He probably should feel at least a bit remorseful for the deception, but he had too much on his mind to bother. He offered the necessary compliments to her form and beauty, suffered through a brief kiss once seated in the coach, and didn't squelch the possibility of a tryst when she hinted a desire for a sultry continuation after the festivities. Perhaps he felt a slight twinge of guilt at the lies. However, he'd do what was necessary to get in, get Ruth and Simon and get out with his neck still connecting his head to his shoulders.

He didn't know Pratt, or at least he didn't remember ever meeting him. Without Gus or Keelan whispering names and facts in his ear, he was a ship with no beacon to guide him in these treacherous waters. In hindsight, leaving Keelan behind might not have been the best decision. Although her disguise would have made it difficult to utilize her knowledge.

Keelan crowded his mind for most of the trip. Her actions, her words. She denied any subversive role in Simon's capture or Hall's near capture by the British with such sincerity. So *very* convincing.

He wanted to believe her.

He wanted to trust her.

But there was still a small uneasy feeling poking at his conscience. What if she was so good at duplicity, that he'd been completely fooled? She could have been deceiving him from the moment they'd met. Visions assaulted him both in sleep and awake... her eyes flashing and defiant, confident and sure, her lips soft and pliant, her breath hungry and passionate. Floating like a water nymph in a lake... Why did that one keep recurring?

Her stories were dubious, her explanations, implausible. It was dangerous to believe her. He groaned inwardly. But it was also difficult to resist her, and hard, even impossible, to ignore her.

Gus had parted company a mile back. He was to tether Juliet in a secluded copse of trees and hide in the brush closer to the barn until Landon signaled him. The carriage jolted to a stop and Landon descended and turned to take Annette's hand as she alighted.

Carriages clustered in front of Leon Pratt's mansion. The columns in front shone with a coat of fresh paint. Tantalizing aromas wafted from somewhere, probably a kitchen house behind the main mansion. Beyond the three-story home was a small lake, then rows of slave cabins. A stable stood in the shade of several large trees. It was likely Pratt would lock up Simon in a confined space away from the festivities.

He untied Orion from behind the livery coach. Near the stable was another barn and a few additional outbuildings. If Simon was still alive, chances were that he was locked in one of them. He'd need to locate a key, perhaps two, one for the door and one for the manacles if Simon had been chained.

A stable boy walked up to take his mount. Rather than hand the reins to the boy, Landon nodded to the carriage coming down the lane behind him. "I can take my horse to the stable, it'd probably be best for you to see to that carriage."

"I'll wait here for you, Landon," Annette said, taking a moment to straighten her dress and shake out the wrinkles from the journey.

The boy nodded and released the bridle. Landon walked his horse nonchalantly to the stable. A groom met him at the barn door. He needed more information, but had to take care in the way he inquired.

"I can put your horse up for ya, sir," the man said.

"I'd be obliged." He handed him the reins. "This is a mighty fine piece of land. Mr. Pratt has seen it tended superbly."

The groom beamed with pride. "Yessuh, he do. Dis plantation be the largest in the Lowcountry."

"I'm afraid I know very little about working the land. I'm a merchant ship captain and spend most of my days on the water. I see you have several barns and sheds in back." He gestured and made a show of turning and perusing the area. "A nice lake and two fine barns."

The groom nodded. "Yessuh, soon filled with the finest rice and tobacco in the Lowcountry. The tobacco is dried in them barns there, after harvest."

"Are they filled now, then?"

The groom bit back a smile and shook his head. "No suh, the tobacco ain't been cut yet, it still growin' in the field out yonder."

"I see, so all those tobacco barns and outbuildings are empty now."

The groom shuffled his feet. "Well, most of dem is empty."

Landon turned his attention back to his horse and loosened the girth strap. "I heard a big commotion on the waterfront today.

Something about a big hulk of a slave named Simon finally being caught. Heard he was Pratt's."

There was a heavy silence behind him. He turned back to the groom who was studying his feet. "Dat so?"

Landon glanced out the open back door of the barn toward the sheds. "If I was a betting man, and I bet another gentleman that I would find Simon in the second outbuilding, would I win the bet?" Landon shifted and although he wanted to observe the groom closely for a flicker of emotion that would give him away, kept his back turned during the silence.

The man's voice hitched up a tiny bit. "Well, suh, I can't say nothin', but I'd sure not bet against ya." He began to brush Orion's coat.

"How can a wooden barn door hold a big man like that?" Landon asked.

"Oh, he ain't goin' nowhere, suh. If he runs, his wife and boy will pay fer it an' he know it."

"I see." That made sense. No need to locate manacle's keys, then. Good. "I'd appreciate it if you'd put my horse up in the stall closest to the back door of the stable, if you would," Landon said, straightening his coat and wiping off his boots. "He tends to get a bit testy around other horses."

"Yessuh," the groom replied, leading Orion away.

He'd have to wait until dark to slip away and free them. From his hiding place, Gus should have a good view of the barns and smaller outbuildings; he'd know, or at least have a solid hunch where Simon was being held, and with luck, Ruth as well.

* * *

LANDON HAD AVOIDED Pratt after the initial introductions, but every time he checked, Pratt's eyes glowered at him, as did those of the men stationed near the doors. So much for clandestinely blending in with the other guests. Earlier today, it had seemed to be a good idea to travel light with just Gus; four people on two horses would be miles away before men could be gathered and horses saddled for a chase. Now he wasn't so sure. An uneasy sensation twisted in his gut.

Something wasn't right.

Had Simon been forced to tell them about Fynn's Freedom Runner network and Landon's involvement? If they knew about the human cargo smuggled in the hidden section of the *Desire's* hold...

He cursed under his breath. He'd seen Annette's invitation as an easy way on to the property. The plan was to socialize and mingle for a short time, then leave when the party goers would move outside. An outdoor dance floor had been installed for dancing by torchlight. It would be easy enough to slip away after dark, find Simon and disappear into the shadows.

Annette was chatting with three elderly matrons seated on a cluster of chairs near a window. Perfect. It was easy to extricate himself from the conversation by offering to bring back refreshments. While doing so, he'd peruse the layout of the house and servant's entrance. If their plan went bad, he'd need to get out quickly.

At least Keelan was safely hidden away. That woman burrowed under his skin faster than a hungry tick. He'd accepted that he'd married her; too many people confirmed it. To be honest, he'd accepted that fact even before Annette's verification. There was something familiar about Keelan, although he wasn't sure what. Her posture? She was small in stature, but in unguarded moments, she held her head like a queen. Perhaps it was her courage and determination; although both could be misunderstood for stubborn persistence and pride.

Loyalty? It was obvious she would have defended Daniel Hunter to her death. He paused. Daniel had done the same for her. He'd been jealous of the man, convinced they were lovers. Listening to Keelan's stories about the man from her childhood had made it clear to him that Mr. Hunter had been a mentor, a tutor, and a friend. He'd been wrong about him.

Keelan. It would be so easy to fall in love with her, so easy to take her into his arms, so easy to give her access to his fragile heart. If only he could trust her. Had she truly loved him? Did she still? It could have all been an act. A good spy might be able to fool him, especially if she were as smart and beautiful as Keelan. Yet the way she kissed him, the way she looked at him, the way she fit in his arms... those were things that were hard to fake. He hated the way his memories eluded him, forcing his mind to fill with paranoid questions and idiotic assumptions. He needed to remember.

Fleeting pictures of her invaded the privacy of his thoughts at all hours of the day and night. Keelan laughing and dancing, sparring in her boy's breeches, naked on his bed, her eyes hooded with passion. The feel of her lips against his felt right. Her scent drew him to her and when he breathed her in, he was in a familiar place like... home.

One part didn't fit, and it vexed him. Fynn had instilled in Landon a deep seated repugnance for slavery from the time Landon was twelve years old. So then, why would he marry a woman who owned both slaves and a plantation? Unless... *unless* she had kept that information from him until they married. He shook his head, confused. Until he remembered everything, he wouldn't completely trust her.

He'd have to stay vigilant.

"May I offer you a glass of Madeira, sir?"

His shoulders stiffened at the voice. *No, it couldn't be*... He whirled and almost collided with the tray in Keelan's arms.

"What the devil are you doing here?" he whispered angrily. He'd already been here well over an hour. How was it he hadn't noticed her before now? Keelan wore a house slave's skirt and blouse with her hair pinned up beneath a simple, ruffled cotton cap. Not a single tendril was exposed.

She lifted a decanter and carefully poured wine into a glass, talking in a low voice as she did so. "I'm here to warn you that Pratt knows about you and the Freedom Runners. He plans to hang you with Simon and Ruth tonight. You have to leave. I've instructed the groom to ready Orion. Go. Now."

Landon sucked in a breath. "Blast it." She stopped pouring the wine and reached for the half-filled glass. He gestured for her to fill it, giving them more time to talk. "I might have been able to fight my way out alone, but I don't see how you can escape with me unless you know how to do something dangerous with that wine carafe."

"I just might." A hint of a smile tugged the corners of her mouth. "I have a plan for my escape, there's no need to concern yourself about me."

How could he possibly focus on freeing Simon if he also had to worry about her? "Keelan, you shouldn't have come here." He almost wished the carafe was filled with something stronger.

"Hush and listen to me," she whispered, handing him the wine. "Ronnie and I have planned a diversion. You'll have to play along. I must warn you that—"

"Oh, *there* he is!" The high pitched voice behind him reminded him of Conal's Great Aunt Celia, a tall, thin woman with a nose like a hawk and a voice that could be heard across the Indian Ocean.

Landon took a sip of wine, turned and choked on it. Approaching him with mincing little steps was Ronnie in a gray silk ball gown, a fan dangling from his wrist. The boy's dark hair had been delicately pinned on top of his head, with a slender tendril left to hang on each side of his face. Landon's gaze moved to the pink cheeks, then the bodice. He had a fichu tucked into the front, covering... was that a slight curve of a *bosom*? A long lace hem brushed the floor, probably covering his boots. Landon took a gulp of wine, at a complete loss for words. It was almost too much to take in.

Behind him, Keelan whispered, "This is your sister, Veronica." She was silent a moment. "Recognize the dress?"

The smile in her voice made him scrutinize Ronnie. A vision of the same dress on an auburn-haired beauty drifted into his mind. In his vision, she had her back to him and was facing a moonlit lake and sipping wine. Was it her? Was it Keelan? He'd followed her into the garden that night. He had a reason for doing so. What was it?

"Actually... I think I do remember the dress." They had danced a waltz in the moonlight. She'd been irritated with him. Why?

Keelan caught her breath behind him. "You do?"

Perhaps he'd tell her about the memory later, if he wasn't dangling by his neck from the end of a rope.

A memory flashed. *She'd had another suitor.* His tall, lanky frame pushed its way to the front of Landon's mind. She'd been avoiding the man. She hadn't wanted to *marry* him. A jolt flashed through his chest. Garrison and Keelan had been engaged. *Engaged.* That meant he'd had every chance to walk away from her; avoid ever seeing her again. Something twisted in his chest, blocking the air from his lungs. He spun to face her. "I think I—"

Yet he hadn't walked away from her. That meant he hadn't been forced to marry Keelan. He must have decided to come back for her. Nohe had a specific plan of action that night. A wispy vision seeped into his mind. She'd taken a glass of wine and disappeared into the garden. He'd follow, ed. Why? The memory faded before he could see what had transpired from that meeting.

"Landon! You left me behind in the livery to arrive all alone." Ronnie swatted Landon's arm with his fan. "Shame on you. I could have been ravaged by highwaymen."

Landon quickly handed his glass back to Keelan so he could remove his handkerchief and cover his mouth to keep the cough from becoming a bark of laughter. Where did Ronan acquire this sudden talent for dramatics?

"Are you all right, dear brother?" Ronnie's eyes twinkled

mischievously even as he pursed his lips. "You should take smaller sips." He took Landon's glass, refilled by Keelan, and handed it back to him. "Maybe this will help calm your guilty conscience."

"I don't believe any amount of wine can help me at this point," Landon mumbled.

Pratt's nasally voice drifted up from behind them. "And who do I have the pleasure of welcoming into my humble home?" Landon stepped aside to allow a silver-haired, round-shouldered man to move in close enough to converse. Leon Pratt dabbed his lips with a handkerchief. He gave Keelan no mind as he descended upon Landon and Ronnie.

Landon gestured to Ronnie. "Mr. Pratt, please allow me to introduce my sister, Veronica Hart. Veronica, I present to you Mister Leon Pratt."

Ronnie batted his fan at Pratt. "Oh please, Mr. Pratt, call me Ronnie, everyone else does."

Pratt took Ronnie's hand and kissed it.

"Oh!" Ronnie jolted as if the kiss had been a bee sting.

Landon coughed into his handkerchief and received a sharp elbow in the ribs from Keelan.

Ronnie blinked. "Goodness! Where are my manners? I was just so taken by your... countenance... that I almost forgot them. How silly of me." Ronnie sank into a wobbly curtsy. "It's a delight to meet you, sir."

Pratt actually blushed. He puffed his chest out and gave Ronnie a closed lip smile, likely because he lacked a full set of teeth. "The pleasure is distinctly mine, Miss Ronnie. May I escort you to the dining hall? I have a most talented cook who has put out a magnificent spread of culinary delights."

"I'd love to!" Ronnie smiled and opened his fan. "My, but these summer days are getting warmer, aren't they?"

Pratt offered Ronnie his arm. "Indeed, normally, we'd be off to Summerville after the party to enjoy cooler climes by now, but I've been delayed a few days." He patted Ronnie's hand. "Which was fortuitous, since it enabled me to have made your delightful acquaintance."

Ronnie fanned himself almost viciously as Pratt led him away. "Oh, you flatter me too much, Mr. Pratt." He turned and glared at Keelan and Landon, then jerked his head, signaling for them to follow.

Pratt's gravelly voice drifted back to them. "Please, Miss Ronnie, I'd be honored if you would call me Leon. After we've had a bite, I hope you will allow me to show you my roses, I have a most splendid garden, indeed."

"Wonderful! I'm sure my brother will agree to be my chaperone." Another over the shoulder glare.

Landon expelled a deep breath and followed. He could think of no scenarios where this ended well.

None at all.

CHAPTER 16

S o far, the charade was working.

Making herself as small and inconspicuous as possible, Keelan moved around people conversing in the ballroom and headed for the kitchen where she could spy on Landon and Ronnie through the door to the dining room.

"What kind of wine is that, little miss?"

Keelan froze, her heart in her throat. She'd been so focused on getting to the kitchen, she hadn't noticed Jared and Sarah Grey. She'd known them as her uncle and aunt all her life, because Jared was Commodore Grey's younger brother. Commodore Grey had raised her. Actually, he had kidnapped her when she was a toddler and brought her home for Daniel and Slaney to raise. Her cousin Brendan discovered her true identity in Uncle Fynn's diary a couple of weeks ago. That was when they learned she was Conal O'Brien's lost sister.

Jared and Sarah Grey were not legally related to her, although they were unaware of that fact, and at the moment, Keelan had no way of proving it to them. She also didn't know if Jared would stand in the way of her being with Landon as he had in the past. He'd constantly urged her father to push her into marriage with

Pratt. When she had told Uncle Jared she planned to marry Landon, he had locked her in her room after telling her that he would find someone more suitable.

Of course, running into Uncle Jared now wouldn't be a problem if Landon would simply remember he'd asked her to be his wife. *And* if they'd been married in a church, rather than performing an ancient handfast ceremony on the *Seeker,* in the middle of the ocean. *Gah!*

Landon now believed she owned slaves as well as a plantation. Here was her chance to find out if Papa had truly left Twin Pines to her as Uncle Jared predicted, or if she'd been eliminated from Papa's will, as Papa had said.

How should she ask?

She could simply inquire if he was the new master of Twin Pines. Or at least the land, since the house apparently had burned down. Yes. That's what she would do. She opened her mouth, then paused. Her British accent would draw attention here. When she posed as a Persian, folks didn't question her voice, mostly because many weren't sure what a Persian should sound like. For that matter, neither did she. Daniel had forged ahead with confident bravado in his disguise and she had followed in the same confident manner and everything had gone well.

But now, her uncle and aunt would surely notice her voice and would instantly recognize it, and then her, even with the dye on her skin. It might be best to change her accent and tone. Why couldn't she think faster? She poured a glass of wine while she thought about the best tact to take. In her distracted state, she poured the stream of wine over the glass and onto her tray. She pulled the carafe up quickly to cease the flow, then tried again, drawing Jared's attention back to her. Drat. It was even more difficult to ignore Uncle Jared's perusal, since he stood so close and seemed to be studying her every move.

"You have a familiar face. Do you belong to Pratt?" He bent down to study her more closely.

Pratt had tried to marry her, most likely to get Twin Pines than anything else. Belong to him? Absolutely *not*. Not ever. Not as a servant or a wife or a...

His question drew his wife's attention and now she was looking at her. *Oh dear.* Aunt Sarah would certainly notice her voice. Refusing to answer would be rude and insubordinate. Keelan kept her head lowered and shoulders rounded. Thankfully, Sarah's attention was temporarily captured by the wine and she accepted the stem from Keelan and sipped.

A British accent wouldn't do. Perhaps French? Spanish? Panic began to bubble inside her chest. All she could do was shake her head 'no'.

No. I do not belong to Pratt.

"Well, out with it girl," Uncle Jared said in frustration.

"She's a mute, dear," Aunt Sarah said gently. "See how she grasps her throat? That's a sign that she cannot speak."

She'd been grasping her throat?

Aunt Sarah patted Keelan's arm. "It's alright, child. Just go about your duties. Thank you for the wine." She smiled sweetly and Keelan's stomach took another guilty twist. Aunt Sarah had always been so kind to her, she hated deceiving the woman.

Unfortunately, she wasn't able to ask Jared about Twin Pines. Drat, again. That information could have removed one more bone of discord between Landon and her, especially if the plantation belonged to Jared. Not wanting to put her disguise in any more jeopardy, she bobbed a quick curtsy and once again made her way to the back of the house.

Under the pretense of cleaning the spilled wine off her tray, she entered the kitchen, placed the tray on the table, grabbed a rag and wiped it. Seeing a plate of canapes, she swapped the tray for the plate and headed for the dining room, hoping she wasn't too late.

"My, you have a healthy appetite, Miss Ronnie," Pratt was saying.

"You'd think I never fed her," Landon responded, a sardonic twist to his mouth.

Ronan had a plate piled with food even as he was eating a small tea cake with his fingers. He turned his attention to Landon. "You don't have a cook half as talented as Leon's," he said before stuffing the rest of the tea cake into his mouth.

Pratt accepted the compliment with a puffed chest and added a sweet roll to both his plate and Ronnie's.

The boy's eyes lit up. "Thank you, you are so *very* kind, Leon."

Keelan gave an inward snort of derision. Kind was the one thing Leon Pratt was *not*. Movement in the corner of her eye alerted her attention. Pratt's men had moved closer to the dining room doorway and now leaned against it like two twin pillars. There was a coiled tenseness about their posture that betrayed their casual stance. Her mind raced with options. The three of them needed to get past those men unnoticed so they could slip away before Pratt decided to have his men take Landon. It was likely the only thing preventing that from happening this moment was Pratt's sudden infatuation with "Veronica."

"Do finish your story, Miss Ronnie," Pratt gushed. "You had reached the part in the play when the hero reaches for his sword as the pirate jumps from the yardarm."

"Oh, yes," Ronnie exclaimed, stepping closer to one of Pratt's guards. "Our hero reaches across his body and grabs the handle of his sword." While holding his plate in his left hand, Ronnie imitated the move with his right. "Then he pulls it from his scabbard so quickly, all you could see was a flash of silver!" Ronnie flung his arm wide in an arching blow left to right, catching the guard square in the nose with the back of his fist.

The move caught Pratt's man by surprise and he stumbled back into the hall with a muffled shout, holding his nose with both hands.

"Oh dear!" Ronnie cried. He clutched his hand to his chest. "Oh, Landon, I fear I may have broken my hand!" Keelan wasn't sure how he did it, but Ronnie managed to appear as if he would break into tears any second.

Landon sprang forward. "Now Ronnie, don't panic. Let's have a look." He took ahold of Ronnie's elbow. "Perhaps you should sit."

Looking every bit as though he was about to break into tears, Ronnie gestured at the man cursing under his breath in the hall. "I'm terribly sorry. He was standing so still and quiet, I didn't even notice he was there."

Pratt smiled at Ronnie. "Don't apologize, my dear." He whirled and stared hard at the man holding his nose. "If he was *doing his job correctly*, he wouldn't have gotten in your way."

His man ducked his head and reached into his pocket to pull out a handkerchief to staunch the blood streaming from his nose and the tears from his eyes.

Ronnie's eyes widened. "Is that... is that... b... b... blood?" Ronnie collapsed in Landon's arms, the plate of food still gripped in his hand.

"Oh, my!" Pratt exclaimed. He fastened his glare on the bleeding man. "For God's sake, man, get out of here until you can make yourself presentable to my guests!"

The guard nodded and disappeared into the kitchen. One down, one to go.

Landon scooped Ronnie up in his arms. "Perhaps you have a bedroom where I can take my sister while she's indisposed?"

"By all means." Pratt led them toward the stairs.

Landon paused and addressed Keelan. "Would you mind coming along to attend to her needs?"

She dropped a quick curtsey. "Of course, sir." She followed the men upstairs.

Pratt led them into a bedroom and hastened to light a lamp. Keelan noted that the second guard had followed them and now lingered by the door.

Landon addressed Pratt. "She will probably need some water, a clean cloth and an extra chamber pot."

Pratt cleared his throat and waved his hand at the guard. "Hawkins, go fetch what is needed."

Keelan let a quiet sigh of relief. With both guards otherwise engaged, they can now focus on their escape.

Landon gently placed Ronnie on the bed. "Thank you, Mr. Pratt. I'm sure my sister will be very grateful for your hospitality and discretion. She so hates to make a public spectacle like this. I'm sure she'll be mortified when she wakes."

Pratt cleared his throat. "I assure you, not a word of this will be mentioned."

"Thank you. I'm sure Veronica will appreciate your discretion." Landon turned back to Ronnie and placed his hand on the boy's forehead. "Please don't let us detain you any longer from your guests. I'm sure they eagerly await your company."

"Yes, well... yes." Pratt clasped his hands behind his back and stepped toward the door. "I do apologize for the ineptitude of Tucker. Stay as long as you wish."

Once Pratt closed the door, Ronnie jumped off the bed and Keelan frantically worked at the buttons on the back of the dress.

"We have to get you both out of here, now," she said. "I'm still unsure if Pratt is convinced Ronnie's your sister." While Keelan unbuttoned the gown, Ronnie finished what was left of the plate of food he'd wedged between his body and Landon's when he collapsed.

Landon strode to the window and flicked back a curtain to peer outside. "If we make it out of here alive, I'm going to kill both of you for putting yourselves in this... this... *situation*."

Ronnie peeled the front of the dress down, releasing his rolled-up shirt which Keelan had used to create a false bosom. "If we hadn't put ourselves in this *situation*, you'd be hanging from a rope tonight." After he shimmied out of the silver silk, he pulled his shirt over his head. "Even the fires of hell can't heat a man faster than a tightly cinched dress." He kicked the garment away from his feet, wiped his brow with his sleeve, then picked up the fan and fanned his chest. After noticing the quizzical expression on Landon's face, he blushed and dropped the fan back on the bed as if it were a hot coal.

Landon gave a soft snort of laughter and shook his head. A movement outside drew his attention. "Pratt has posted a man beneath the window." He huffed out a breath.

Keelan opened the door and peered out. "Quickly!" She gestured for them to move into the room across the hall. "Perhaps you can climb out this one instead."

"I'm not leaving without you," Landon gritted out.

"I'll sneak out the servant's entrance and meet you where we hid Ole Poke. Ronnie with take you. Go!" She gave him a push.

Landon and Ronnie darted across the hall. The voices of a woman and Pratt's other guard drifted up the stair. There was no time to follow or dash down the hall to the servant's staircase. She caught her breath. The door across the hall was still swinging closed as the two servants cleared the top step.

She hopped into the hall. "Thank goodness!" Keelan pressed a hand to her chest. "I feared you wouldn't be in time." The door across the hall eased shut. She snatched the chamber pot and bolted back into the bedroom and slammed the door. There was no place to hide or escape.

Blast it, she was trapped.

The silver ball gown was still in a puddle on the floor. Could she possibly make it out of the house posing as Veronica? She bit her fingernail. It was too great a risk. There was too much disparity in their appearance. Hopefully, Landon and Ronnie could make it into the woods behind the barn. The image of Landon swinging from a rope sent a shiver rippling across her shoulders. She shook her head. That would not happen. It couldn't. She wouldn't let it.

She needed to make the servants believe there was an indisposed woman in this room. She stared down at the chamber pot still in her arms. After coughing loudly several times, she opened the door a crack and reached out for the rags and water bucket. The thick chested man handed them to her silently. She nodded her thanks, careful to avoid eye contact, and closed the door again.

Keelan picked up her gown, and couldn't hold back a small smile at the memory of the last time she'd worn it. That particular night, she had escaped the stifling air of the house at Twin Pines and escaped to the lake. The moon had illuminated the sky that night, creating shadows everywhere. Landon had followed her and tricked her into a waltz. They'd danced in the garden and he had teased, then goaded her into kissing him. She'd never been able to back down from a challenge and when he raised a very sardonic brow and said he doubted she knew how to instigate a kiss... well, she'd shown him she could indeed.

It was *that* moment, the veil between them had slipped away. Gone was her mask of indifference, her trepidations and fear of being used and manipulated for fun. Gone, too, was the cocky, teasing Landon Hart, who hid his intentions behind mockery and challenges. In its stead was a man who drew her to him, bared his heart and asked her to end her charade and choose him rather than the man she'd considered a safer option. He'd asked her to elope with him that night.

She sighed, unable to prevent the tug of longing that followed that last memory. The idea of eloping with Landon had made her heart happy. Then, of course, her cousin spotted them and sent the entire house into an uproar. Such was her life, when in close proximity of Captain Landon Hart. A constant uproar.

Keelan smoothed the gown across the corner of the bed, making sure it was visible if someone was determined to peek inside. She stuffed some cushions under the covers. It wouldn't fool anyone for long, but she only needed a few precious minutes. All she required now was a little water in the chamber pot. That done, she balanced it against her hip and sidled out of the door, closing it firmly.

She started for the servants' stair, then paused and spoke to the man at the door. "Mr. Hart requested us to leave him and his sister alone for a while. You may tell Mr. Pratt that Miss Veronica is awake but terribly embarrassed and will not return to the party. Mr. Hart told me to tell you that he will seek out Mr. Pratt in a couple of hours once his sister has fallen asleep. She is very, very upset at the moment."

The man gave her a nod and a thin smile. His expression resembled that of a cat holding a trapped mouse under his paw. She swallowed and headed down the stair, careful to avoid looking over her shoulder to see if he still stood at his post. No doubt, he'd quickly departed to find his employer and relay the information. Trapping Landon upstairs would fall right in with their plans to kill him.

Keelan walked straight through the busy kitchen and out the back door. Had anyone considered delaying her, the chamber pot she held in front of her along with her wrinkled nose would have discouraged them. It wasn't until she rounded the corner of the first barn that she released her breath. Slipping inside, she noticed Orion in the corner stall.

A trickle of unease ran up her spine. He shouldn't still be in the barn. Landon and Ronnie should have taken him and fled the plantation. A quick glance told her that his girth strap had been tightened, and he was ready to ride. If she could manage to sneak Orion from the barn, then she could easily catch up with Landon and Ronnie.

"Keelan."

Startled, she whirled to find Ronnie standing behind her. "Where's Landon?" She sliced her gaze past him. Had he been caught?

Ronnie pointed to the second shed a couple hundred yards

from the barn. "He's trying to pick the lock. Simon's in there. He has me keeping an eye out for him."

A harsh voice interrupted the quiet of the barn. "He should not have sent a boy to do a man's job."

At the sound of the strange voice, the hair on the back of Keelan's neck tingled and her breath caught in her throat. The thick bulk of a man stepped behind Ronnie and put a pistol to the boy's head. Two more appeared at his flanks and by the widening of Ronnie's eyes, there were probably more behind her. She recognized the man holding the pistol to Ronnie's head as the guard who'd been outside the bedroom door, Hawkins. Her shoulders sagged. He must have followed her, rather than locate Pratt. She'd failed.

Hawkins leered at her. "I've been trailing Hart since he made port. I knew he'd lead me to you eventually, Keelan Grey. It wasn't until he told you to accompany him upstairs that I realized who you really were."

Panic pierced Keelan's chest. Then where was Landon?

"I have no use for the woman, Hawkins." Pratt's voice came from behind her. "You may take her after your job is completed. I must return to my guests."

"I'll take care of it as we agreed," Hawkins said, pulling back the hammer.

CHAPTER 17

With her wrists bound in front of her, and her back against the side of the moving wagon, Keelan worked harder to wiggle her hands out of the ropes. The men hadn't searched her as they had Ronnie. Using the short, thick blade hidden in her waistband, she'd spent the past several minutes sawing through her bindings. Every bump and jolt rattled her frame and jarred her bones. Twice her blade slipped and sliced her skin. Thankfully, Ronnie somewhat blocked her activity from view. She could barely make out his face in the diminishing light. His panicked stare met hers and she wanted so badly to reassure him with a smile or a steady look, but the best she could do was a stoic glare and nod. "Stay strong, Ronan," she whispered, using his given name. She couldn't bring herself to make promises she couldn't keep, and right now the only promise she could make the boy was that she'd fight for their lives until her last breath.

Ronnie's Adam's apple jerked up and down as he returned her nod. His skin rippled along his jaw, and he straightened, almost as if he'd read her thoughts. They were now about a mile or so away from the stable, in a wooded area far from the main house and the eyes of the party guests.

A sense of dread seeped into her stomach. Whatever Hawkins and his men were going to do, they were going to do it well away from any witnesses, that was a certainty. The dim light of a fire flickered through the trees, and it wasn't long before they reached it. The blaze crackled and burned near a large oak. Emotion tangled in her throat and the sharp pain of panic sliced her chest open at the sight before her.

Two negro bodies crumpled together against a third form near the trunk. Dangling from the tree's branches were three ropes. The hard knot in her throat tightened at the sight of a familiar pair of polished black boots. It wasn't until the wagon stopped that she had a clearer view. Her mouth dropped open in a silent scream as she recognized Simon, Ruth and... Landon.

No! A trickle of blood ran from a gash on his temple. His eyes were closed. A cry escaped her throat, and she choked on a harsh sob. They'd failed. They'd failed to save them. They'd failed all three of them. She let her head fall to her knees as another sob threatened to shudder through her chest. Next to her, Ronnie froze in horror. His shoulder jerked into hers as he was pulled out of the wagon.

"Toss one more rope up there," Hawkins ordered, yanking Ronnie toward the tree. "We have a fourth."

Keelan's head snapped up and hope flared. That meant they hadn't hung them, not yet anyway. She fixed her stare on Landon's chest. It moved. He wasn't dead. He wasn't dead!

Landon stirred then, moaning. He rolled over and blinked his eyes open. Cursing, he attempted to sit up, but one of the men raised his booted foot and pushed him back against the tree trunk. Another shoved Ronnie in the direction of the captives where he landed on his knees next to Landon's feet, his eyes wide with fear.

Disarm, distract or delay. Daniel's instructions from long ago, during her early training. "You can't hang him!" Keelan cried. "He's only a boy!"

Hawkins pulled her from the wagon. "He'll be hanged for aiding runaways."

She'd slipped the knife into her sleeve and hid the cut ends of the severed rope in her fists. They'd underestimated her, and she'd make sure they'd regret it. They were few against many, but if they were going to die tonight, she'd take as many with her as she could.

"And our family will hunt you down," she replied, glaring her hatred while she took in her surroundings. Hawkins had a knife at his waist and a holstered pistol on his right thigh. She'd reach for the pistol first, when she had the opportunity. Most of his men carried similar weapons, although some also had a rifle nearby or strapped to their saddle.

Hawkins laughed. "You'll be in no position to tell anyone once Gampo gets ahold of you, and I'll be long gone, my pockets jingling with coin." He reached up and stroked a strand of her hair. "Although, I heard that the price on your head is substantially higher if I bring you to Captain Gampo still alive."

"Let her go!" Landon's face darkened with fury; he struggled against his bindings.

Keelan glanced at the pistol. She'd have to be quick. Stumble into him, dip, and grab the handle before he realized what she was doing. It had to be fast and smooth.

Hawkins grabbed her chin and continued as if Landon hadn't spoken. "Or, I can take a piece of your scalp, instead." He nudged her forward before she could execute her plan. "Move a bit closer. It would be a shame if you missed all the fun."

Well, closer was better. With the hardest part of their duties behind them, Pratt's men relaxed. Some sat near the fire, others milled around the horses, waiting.

He shoved her toward one of his men. "Keep an eye on her."

The man leered, a gaping, yellow-toothed grin. He smelled of horse dung and whiskey, and she hoped he'd imbibed the alcohol recently. As he started to drag her toward the fire; she stumbled and fell to her knees. When he reached down to haul her to her feet, she drove the small blade she'd used to cut her ties into his shoulder, then snatched the pistol from his belt. His eyes widened and before he could shout out, the pistol caught him square on the chin. She grabbed his blade as he fell and threw it at the tree. It imbedded in the trunk less than six inches from Ronan's side. All he needed to do was grab it and hold it tightly enough for Landon to cut his bindings.

"Don't stand there, like idiots!" Hawkins shouted. "Stop her! Just don't kill her."

She pulled the knife from the wounded man and threw it at the closest gunman. It imbedded in his shoulder and his weapon dropped to the ground, his arm now useless. The others paused and eyed her warily when she pulled her stiletto from her boot.

Freed from his bonds, Landon jumped the nearest ruffian and shoved him into the fire. The man screamed and flailed while another hopped forward to pull him out.

The camp erupted into chaos.

Some of Hawkins' men descended on Landon, others froze in panic, and still others dove for cover. Landon pulled the blade from the trunk and plunged it into a gunman's chest; Keelan's stiletto sank into the back of another who had his rifle trained on Landon. She shot a third.

Although still bound, Simon staggered to his feet and with a bellow like a wounded bull, plowed his head and shoulder into a fourth man. Ruth kicked out with her legs, tripping another. Figures lunged and yelled in the general mayhem, the glow of the fire creating grotesque shadows that danced against the surrounding trees.

She was out of weapons and had lost track of Hawkins. Frantically, she glanced around for something she could use to defend herself. She grabbed a short thick branch, but before she could swing it, her head was jerked back and she was thrown to the ground, then her wrists clamped in manacles. The cold steel of a blade pressed against the tender skin beneath her jaw.

"Hart!" Hawkins shouted. A pistol shot cracked. The camp stilled. Their little rebellion was over in seconds. A sinking dread settled in the pit of her stomach and she wanted to scream for Landon to fight.

Landon jerked away from one man and lunged toward them, but was brought down by two more. He glared at Hawkins and spoke through gritted teeth, his voice low and promising. "Harm her and I'll kill you."

Hawkins yanked her to her knees and returned the tip of his blade to her throat. By the sting, it had broken her skin. A warm, slow trickle of blood crept down her neck. "You're in no position to make such ridiculous threats, let alone carry them out." He barked out orders to the five men still standing. "String them up so we can get back to the house. I want my share from Pratt so I can get word to Gampo that I found his prize."

Keelan snarled and struggled to her feet, only to be pushed back to her knees. A wave of dizziness and nausea hit her and she sat back on her heels. Fainting now would not help Landon or the others. This time, they bound his feet as well. Simon and Ronnie were dragged back to the tree near Ruth. Keelan could only watch helplessly.

Hawkins' men, battered and bloodied, reached for the dangling nooses and dropped them around the necks of their four captives. Simon was unconscious; Ruth's lip was split and the one eye that wasn't swollen shut glared at the men in defiance. Blood streamed from Ronnie's nose. Landon's steady blue stare trapped hers and she held it, blocking out everything and everyone else. Her world narrowed until all she could see, feel, and hear was Landon. She didn't even care about her fate in the hands of Gampo. Nothing mattered but her husband, the man of her heart.

Four horses were led up to the tree and the other end of each rope tied to the saddle horn. With the nooses already secured, all that had to be done was to lead the horses away from the tree. The four would be hauled up and off the ground by their necks. Death would not be as fast as a quick drop, but inevitable nonetheless.

Landon's dark hair gleamed a blue-black. Several strands had escaped from the queue during the scuffle. The firelight flickered in his light blue irises along with something else. Something was different.

Absent was the cold, distant countenance of a stranger.

In its place was the familiar look of appraisal and admiration she'd grown to love. The shift in his demeanor radiated to where she stood, filling her with a comforting warmth, even in such a hopeless situation. At that tiny moment in time, it was just the two of them.

"I love you," she whispered.

"I remember," he stated softly, as one of the men tightened the noose around his neck.

Keelan's breath seized in her throat and tears burned in her eyes. He'd come back to her. Her Landon was back.

"I remember you, sparring in the meadow," he continued, voice low and even. "And I remember kissing you in the garden. Your hair was tangled in a bush and I remember thinking that you were the most impetuous and beautiful woman I'd ever met. I decided that day that I'd find a way to make you mine."

The tears dripped from her jaw to her collarbone; her heart filled with a sudden rush of surging joy. They were both about to die, and she should be drowning in fear, but instead she was filled with an incredible lightness.

He remembered her. He remembered *them*.

"I love you, Keelan Hart." Landon said in a firm and clear voice. The shocking blue of his eyes held hers in a gaze that pulsed with confident strength and boundless love.

The men clucked the horses into motion. She would not to break eye contact with her husband and watch the rope tighten around his neck. She would not. If he was going to die tonight, then in her eyes he would see love and devotion that would span the dark crevasse of death.

And one day soon, both Hawkins and Pratt would see her hatred and vengeance. Because she *would* avenge Landon's murder.

The forest grew alarmingly quiet, the crackling fire the only sound. Keelan swallowed a sob. Landon would not see her crumble. He would *not*.

A whisper of metal against leather reached her ears, then almost simultaneously, the men leading the horses grunted and slowly sank to the ground. The horses stopped.

"Wha—" A dirk hit Hawkins' chest and cut off the rest of his sentence.

Ronnie whipped his head around. "It's about time! Where in the blazes have you *been*?" His voice cracked. The last word was nothing more than a squeak.

Keelan peered into the darkness surrounding the fire and blinked. The crew from the *Desire*, all eighty of them, surrounded the clearing. The glint of sabers and pistols in the moonlight was a welcome sight indeed. Half a dozen stepped forward and pulled their blades from the dead men. Keelan recognized them as the crewmen she and Daniel had tutored over the past few weeks. Relief brought on another dizzying wave, and she closed her eyes and nearly wept.

Marcel lifted the noose from his captain's neck. "Well, it took us a bit longer on foot zan we expected," he grumbled. "Zere was only one wagon left to hire."

Gus cut Ronnie's bonds, then turned his weathered face to Landon. "When ye didn't make it back from the party, I struck out for the *Desire* to get some help, but ran into Marcel and the men before I'd gone far." He pulled the boy to his feet. "Who is Keelan Hart?" He took a step toward Keelan. "And why in the name of all that's holy, is Mahdi dressed like a *woman*?"

THE BRAZEN RAYS of early dawn had almost pierced the horizon by the time they neared the outskirts of Charleston. Landon removed his handkerchief to peer at the wound under Keelan's jaw as their wagon rolled toward the city. They were all battered, but alive. Gus held the reins and Ronnie rode behind them on Orion. Simon, Joseph and Ruth were hidden in a coffin-like compartment beneath the wagon's floor. Another dozen sailors sat on the wagon bed to help hide them.

"Pratt is a powerful man in the Lowcountry." Keelan plucked a twig from Landon's hair. "I'm not convinced the sheriff will listen to our tale with an impartial ear."

He gave her a sardonic grin. "Eighty men following us would willingly bear witness if need be. However, tomorrow, I shall deliver to the sheriff a letter detailing tonight's events, signed by the crew. That will have to be good enough." He pulled her closer. "I believe we have outstayed our welcome here, love."

"The lot of us have," she gave a short laugh. "I hear the world is a big place, however. There is much I haven't seen."

"It will be my honor to show it to you, my sweet." He brushed a curl from her face, then leaned forward until their foreheads touched. "Can you forgive me, Keelan, for the torment I've put you through these past few weeks?" The anguish in his voice nearly broke her heart.

She traced a finger along the stubble of his jaw, then down his neck and over his shoulder, marveling at the rigid muscle beneath. "There's nothing to forgive," she whispered through her tears.

He cupped her face in his hands. "I should have believed you.

I should have protected you better. I should have trusted you. I promise to never put you in that kind of danger ever—"

She pressed a finger over his lips and smiled. "Landon Hart, don't make a promise you can't keep."

"My love—"

She silenced him with a kiss.

CHAPTER 18

G us pulled the carriage to a halt with a short, clipped, "Whoa."

Landon and Keelan hopped down to the narrow alley behind The Whistling Pig. Dawn was upon them and they moved with a quiet intensity. Simon, Ruth and Joseph were whisked up to the third floor to join Yanda and her family. They'd been moved off the *Desire* in case Pratt managed to have Landon's ship searched. Keelan hoped Pratt would be too busy putting out fires to send word to the harbormaster demanding such. She and Mrs. Schoen treated their cuts and bruises, and then it was time to say goodbye.

Keelan hugged the softly weeping cook. "I'll miss you, Ruth. I pray you, Simon and Joseph find a better life in Canada."

Ruth sniffled and squeezed her a little harder. "Thank you, Miss Keelan." She stepped back and wiped her eyes with her apron and cleared her throat. "Now don't you forget the way I taught you to make my lemon scones and ham patties."

Keelan smiled. "I won't. Nor will I forget how to make your bannocks or Indian meal cakes." She reached down and gave Joseph's shoulder a little pat. "You watch after your mum."

"Yes, ma'am."

Ruth's soft brown face broke into a smile, even as another tear fell. "God is good," she whispered, "God is so very good."

~~~

AFTER A SHORT DISCUSSION, Landon and Gus decided that it would be best for the Schoens to hand Simon and company off to another Freedom Runner due in to port within the next couple of days. Landon would immediately take the *Desire* back south again as a decoy.

The change of plans meant that they could return their attention to finding Conal, which lightened her heart considerably. She missed her brother and worried about his welfare at the hands of the pirates who captured him and his ship. Given their history with Gampo, she suspected the pirate captain to be behind the kidnapping. The important question was why? The blackguard offered a reward for her, not Conal. Landon guessed he was using Conal as bait, because he knew they'd come after him.

She worried, too, about her maid Slaney, who'd left Charleston for England with the mission to secure information from an old trunk in Keelan's childhood country home. There was no need to do that now, since the discovery of Uncle Fynn's journal and the revelation that Keelan was an O'Brien by birth. By now, Slaney's ship would have deposited her in Philadelphia, where she would have sought a vessel bound for Boston. Keelan took the time to pen several letters to the maid who'd been more like a mother to her, telling her about the recent events. She sent them to various harbormasters in Philadelphia, New York and Boston, hoping one of them would reach Slaney before she set off from America to England. It broke her heart to write about Daniel's death, because it would break Slaney's heart, too. She even sent a letter for Commodore Hall, asking him to inquire after the maid while at port.

Her husband pulled her into his embrace. "The *Desire* is a fast ship when she needs to be. She's stalwart and brave. Most of her cargo has been offloaded, so she'll ride light and nimble." Landon kissed her forehead. "It shouldn't take us long to reach Jamaica."

"And you have a strong, loyal crew," she added, thinking back to the dark expressions she'd seen on their faces when they'd descended on the camp.

"Aye to that."

Keelan, Landon, and Gus found a seat in the Tavern's empty common room and waited for Ronnie to return. The Blue Peter waved atop the mizzen mast of the *Desire*, calling all hands on board. Ronnie, however, had dashed away as soon as they arrived at the tavern, with a shouted excuse that he had to see to something urgent.

Keelan was anxious to return to the *Desire* and the privacy of their cabin. She had a surprise for Landon. She smiled her thanks at Mrs. Schoen when she brought them a couple cups and a pot of tea with sprig of peppermint floating on top. Keelan dropped a hand to her stomach, thankful for the thoughtful gesture, and hopeful she'd not need it for all the weeks to come. "Are you certain Ronnie didn't say where he was going?"

"*Nein*," the woman replied. "Only to tell you dat you must vait for him here."

Keelan reached for a small chunk of cheese, suddenly ravenous. "That seems odd," she said. "He knows no one in Charleston, except us."

Landon shrugged and shook his head, reaching for the tea. His hand stilled immediately when a tankard of ale was plunked down in front of him. Mr. Schoen gave him a quick grin, then spun back toward the bar.

The door to the tavern burst open and cracked against the wall. A frantic clergyman dashed in. Mrs. Schoen jumped, pressed her hand to her chest and blurted something in German that caused Mr. Schoen to jerk to a halt and raise his eyebrows.

The priest gasped for breath; his wiry, white hair stood at all angles, either due to being abruptly roused from slumber without time for a comb or perhaps buffeted that way by an early morning dash through the Charleston streets. "Am I too late?"

"Late for...?" Mr. Schoen reached for an empty tankard.

The priest pierced Mr. Schoen with an agitated look. "The boy said it was urgent. I'm here to perform last rites to a sorry soul, God save 'im."

Ronnie slipped into the tavern and paused behind the priest. He gave Landon and Keelan a sheepish nod, then tapped the priest on the shoulder and whispered loudly. "I din't say the man was *dying*, Father. I said that you can save him from burning in hell."

The priest's wizened face wrinkled even further with confusion as he stared at Ronnie. "What's that you say?"

The boy pointed to Landon. "That man has cleaved unto that woman without the holy blessing of God and the church, Father. The woman is my cousin, and I fear for both their mortal souls. Only you can save them. Will you?"

Keelan's chunk of cheese fell to the table with a soft thunk. For a moment, neither she nor Landon moved a muscle. In both shock and complete disbelief, they stared wide-eyed at Ronnie. Gus broke into a sudden fit of coughing. On the trip back to town, Landon had explained to him that Mahdi was not a Persian boy, but instead his wife by a handfast ceremony, and it was a full minute before Gus's dropped jaw had closed back into place. During the rest of the ride to The Whistling Pig, he'd occasionally cough out a spontaneous chuckle and shake his head. Keelan couldn't wipe the grin from her face if her life depended on it.

The priest pulled out a chair and sat down with a thump. "Oh, dear Lord," he huffed. "My hearing is not as good as it once was." He heaved a breath and licked his lips. "Mr. Schoen, would you see your way clear to parting with a tankard of that fine *beir* of yours? Just a small amount, a bit, a tankard to moisten my parched throat. It'll do these two children of God no good if my words are too dry to reach the good Lord's ears."

Already anticipating the clergyman's needs, Mr. Schoen placed a frothy tankard on the bar and Ronnie put it in front of the priest. After the man had quenched his thirst, he lowered his brows at Landon and sent a slightly more benign smile in Keelan's direction.

"Now then." He picked up his Bible and opened a page marked by a red ribbon, then looked sternly at the two. "Let's get about saving your souls from the devil's greedy claws and marry the two of you before it's too late."

Landon's white teeth flashed a jubilant grin, his eyes sparkling with mirth and love. "An excellent suggestion, Father." Keelan could only laugh. Landon pulled her to her feet, reached for her hands and entwined his fingers with hers.

The priest perused the room. "Now, who gives this woman?"

"I do!" Ronnie hurried to stand next to her. He licked his hand and ran it over his hair, then glanced down and quickly tucked in his shirt. He straightened, giving the priest an earnest nod.

The priest nodded and glanced about. "And who will stand by this man?"

Gus squirmed in his chair, then cleared his throat. "I'd be honored to stand as witness, if you'll have me."

Landon clapped Gus on the shoulder. "Thank you, Gus."

She looked down at her soiled and blood-stained clothing before wrinkling her nose at Landon. "We must be a sight to behold." Although most of the blood had been washed from their hands and faces, their clothes were still dirty and torn, their faces bruised. Her hair probably looked as if someone took a broom to it.

"God loves all his children, whether in rags or riches," the priest mumbled, running his finger over a passage in his Bible.

Landon's voice rumbled in her ear. "You are beautiful in both, but I prefer you in neither."

She gave him a warm smile. A hand squeezed Keelan's arm, and she turned to find Mrs. Schoen presenting a small bouquet of tea roses circling a creamy white magnolia blossom, all held together by a tattered piece of ivory silk.

"Der tea roses," Mrs. Schoen said, "mean remembrance. Magnolia means..." she searched for the right word, "... perseverance."

Keelan kissed the woman's cheek. "Thank you, Mrs. Schoen, they're lovely." She fingered the familiar silk and smiled. The woman touched the corner of her apron to her eye and then bustled over to stand by her husband and sniffle.

Landon grasped her elbow, and she turned to face him. The love in his eyes warmed her soul. Her own welled with joyful tears.

"Had I known Ronan's plan, I'd have brought you a gift," Landon said.

She pulled his hand to her abdomen, unable to wait any longer. "You already have."

๑๛๑

WITH KEELAN IN HIS ARMS, Landon swept into his cabin then kicked the door shut. "Welcome home, Mrs. Hart," he said, smiling broadly.

She looped her arms around his neck. "Home is where ever *you* are, Captain Hart." She sighed and leaned her head on his shoulder. "I never want to leave your arms."

He gave her a loving squeeze. "I see something that might make you leap from them eagerly." There was no mistaking the smile in his voice.

She glanced over her shoulder. "Oh!" She wiggled and Landon laughed as he released her legs, allowing her to slide enticingly down a solid length of muscle and bone. She paused long enough to bestow a quick kiss on his cheek before pulling off her shirt.

She gave the soiled thing a disgusted kick to the corner, then turned her attention on the copper tub. "Mister Marcel, you are a wonderful, wonderful man!"

Landon managed to appear wounded. "Madam, you forget who gives the orders around here. Who do you think planted the seed in his ear?"

Keelan giggled and returned to pepper his face with kisses. "I love you. I love you. I love you," she whispered between each kiss.

Large hands circled her waist, and he pulled her against him for a longer, more languid kiss. Their tongues danced together like lovers, caressing, stroking, probing. She could never tire of this. Again she sent up a prayer of gratitude for *her* Landon's return. With his love lifting her up, she could face anything.

Landon broke the kiss and rested his forehead against hers, his breathing ragged and deep. "You're testing my strength, Madam." He tipped his chin toward the bath. "Unless you take advantage of Marcel's gift now, I'm afraid the water will chill before I allow you another opportunity."

He laced his fingers with hers and lead her to the tub. A lovely sachet of dried jasmine blossoms and spices floated in the water. Landon smiled at Keelan's blissful sigh as she lowered herself into the bath. She reached for the new chunk of citrusy-smelling soap and a sponge, but Landon beat her to them, gently brushing her hands away. To her surprise, he proceeded to wash her, his attention on her skin, one square inch at a time.

"Before my memory returned, I kept having these dreams of a fire-haired vixen sparring in deep meadow grass. Or of a water sprite floating naked on a crystal blue lake," he whispered, his voice gravelly. He stroked away the crusted blood on her neck, then lowered his head to kiss the hollow between her collar bones, making her breath hitch. "But I could never make out her face."

He sponged her chest, the water trickling down between her breasts and over her hardening nipples. He made erotic circles with the sponge before replacing it with his hands. Callused thumbs abraded the sensitive skin, and she closed her eyes, reveling in the delicious scraping sensation that tugged an invisible string behind her navel leading straight through her core. At his light pinch, she arched her back.

His voice dropped. "I couldn't see you, and it was slowing destroying my sanity." His hands disappeared and before she could groan her disappointment, warm water cascaded over her chest. A hot, moist mouth captured her right breast and lathed it with a velvet tongue. Landon sucked her nipple deep into his mouth, causing another vicious tug on that invisible string. He turned his attention to the others breast, and she threaded her fingers into his ebony curls, unable to keep the low moan of pleasure trapped in her chest.

"Landon..."

He hushed her with a soft kiss before pulling her to her feet and continuing the tender cleansing of her body, the sponge reverently stroking her gently healed back, the flat of her stomach and the round curves of her backside. He moved with a determined purpose, as if he was washing away the physical wounds as well as the emotional ones. "I abandoned you, Keelan." The anguish in his voice was palpable, and a band around her chest constricted at his pain. "I promised to bind myself to you body and bone until death parts us, but I didn't."

She cupped his cheek with her hand, but he wouldn't look at her. "That wasn't your fault, Landon," she murmured, trying to calm his agitated demeanor.

He didn't meet her gaze, instead directing his full attention to washing her, making her heart hurt even more. It was as if he was determined to rinse away every painful moment of anger and distrust he'd hurled at her since the accident. Guilt and anguish coated his features. "I put you in danger. I brought you back to Charleston," he said, harsh tones lacing his voice. He pulled a hand over his face, eyes a haunted silver-blue. "Instead of protecting you, I lead you to the very men hunting you!"

"You had no way of knowing that at the time." Every word from his mouth tightened the bands around her chest. She wished she knew how to ease his suffering. She wanted to pull in all inside her body to free him from the guilt and pain.

He swallowed, face pale and drawn. "I almost lost you today."

A vision invaded her mind of Landon, rope around his neck, azure eyes steeped in love and despair and fixed on her. A shiver rippled through her body, although the water was plenty warm. "We almost lost each other, but we didn't. We're here. *Together*. This is where we are supposed to be." She pulled him to her and kissed him, putting every bit of reassurance and love into it as she could. The need to be closer had her removing his shirt to run her hands over the hot skin beneath. "Join me," she breathed.

He doffed his clothes and stepped into the tub. Yet, he stood woodenly, shoulders slumped. She eased the sponge from his hands and proceeded to wash him as he had her caressing sore muscles, rinsing away blood and grime from strong shoulders and powerful legs. Water sluiced down his magnificent body, leaving him gleaming like a sun-kissed god. As she ran her hands over the light coating of crisp hair on his chest, she idly wondered if a man's nipples were as sensitive as a woman's. She experimentally ran her finger around his and was rewarded with a quick inhale. Exploring further, she licked him, then flicked her tongue across it, eliciting a low growl that vibrated under her lips. Sucking them seemed to have a similar affect, and soon Landon's fingers were tangling in her dampened locks. Heat flared in his eyes, warming places low in her belly. Running her hands down his slick torso, she slowly sank to her knees.

He groaned. "Keelan—"

A pearly drop beaded at the blunt head of his arousal. She flicked her tongue across it, eliciting another sharp intake of breath from Landon. She licked him again, more boldly this time.

Although she was unsure of exactly what she was doing, she figured there were very few ways to do it wrong. If the raw craving and need in Landon's expression was any indication, then she was on the right path. Gripping his shaft, she took him more fully into her mouth and sucked lightly on the way back up.

"Good God, Keelan!" Landon's hoarsely whispered inhale made her smile. He curled his hands deeper into her hair.

She looked up. His face was washed with stark need, eyes a smoldering midnight blue. The way he watched her—with heated desire and longing, promises of undying love and devotion— pulled harder at the string behind her navel, causing that delirious ache to spread even lower in her belly. The juncture of her thighs throbbed and grew wetter. She never expected the desire to please him, to feel so sensual and erotic. She pulled him into her mouth again, going deeper and sucking harder this time, squeezing his shaft and twirling her tongue around it as she withdrew.

Landon groaned and sucked in a rattled breath. "If you don't stop, I'll likely go mad." He pulled her up and stepped out of the tub before lifting her into his arms and striding toward the bed, not caring that they were slick with jasmine-and citrus-smelling water.

He lowered her onto the bed, nipping, licking and kissing his way down her body until he was between her thighs. Without warning, he swept his tongue up, parting her folds until he reached that most sensitive spot on her body. Keelan's lungs quit working as a coil of pleasure spiraled up through her center. Landon sucked gently, tightening the coil until it quivered beneath his mouth. She fisted the covers just as he slipped a finger inside her, then a second, stretching her. He pulled them out then swirled them back inside then out again, creating a rhythm that had her thrashing in near-delirium.

"Please, Landon—I need you," she panted, certain something was going to burst soon if he didn't replace his fingers with the thick length he was cruelly withholding from her. She was right. The climax hit her like an earthquake, the coil vibrating and whipping through her body like a hurricane.

Landon hummed in pleasure. "That's it, love. That's it." He caressed her breast, then just as the waves of delight began to subside, Landon set his mouth to her again, sending an aftershock through her that curled her toes. Probably permanently.

Landon's voice was husky with emotion. "Forgive me, my love, for putting you through—"

She pressed her fingers over his mouth. "There is nothing to forgive. You are my heart and my soul. I will fight for you always until the day I die."

"I'll never doubt it," he murmured. "Never again. We were meant to be together, you and I. I knew it the moment I kissed that impish hellion tangled in that garden bush."

He kissed her deeply, pressing the thick head of his erection against her slick opening. A slight shift sent him slipping inside, and they both gasped at the sudden joining. Heat from his skin seeped into her and she kissed him back almost frantically. He whispered against her mouth, "You are my light and my breath."

Pulling away, she smiled into those sapphire eyes filled with primal need, boundless love and undying troth. She locked her ankles behind his back and pulled him in deeper. "Welcome home, Captain Hart."

🐚

IN THE FOLLOWING MONTHS, stories were passed around, mostly with hushed tones and whispers in The Whistling Pig, that among the small band of pirates who had stolen Conal O'Brien's ship was a pirate heiress. She sought a secret treasure that had been hidden almost a hundred years earlier by her great-grandparents, Calico Jack Rackham and Anne Bonny. The rumors were never confirmed (since the Ahern-Hart Merchant fleet wisely never returned to Charleston) but neither were they refuted.

FOLLOW Conal O'Brien's journey in <u>If You Give A Pirate A Treasure,</u> the next book in The Pirates & Petticoats Series.

TO RECEIVE an email alert for the next release: http://chloeflowers.com/contact/

A PORTION OF PROFITS GO TO THE NATIONAL BREAST CANCER FOUNDATION.

SNEAK PEEK: IF YOU GIVE A PIRATE A TREASURE

SNEAK PEEK

June 1811
New Orleans

S tanding among the charred debris of his family's boarding house in New Orleans, Bernard Sauvage lifted a blackened marble box from the rubble. Nearby, his sons as well as his late brother's children were salvaging what they could, shifting bricks and burned beams.

The smoke-scented morning was hushed by tragedy; they'd lost everything.

Bernard shifted the box in his hand well enough to remove the lid, then sucked in his breath. Two roughly cut emeralds rested on a stack of letters. He stared for a moment before brushing them with his fingertips, half expecting them to dissolve into dust.

They were real.

He fingered through the yellowed parchment. The first letter was dated almost 100 years ago. He scanned it and raised his eyebrows in shock at the signature.

It had been written by the notorious female pirate, Anne Bonny.

Bernard moved to an upturned water trough and sat to read. A short time later, he replaced the letters in the marble box along with the emeralds. The lady pirate hinted that she'd hidden a fortune in jewels just before she and the crew of the *Gallant* had been captured.

It was a risk, but if he could find this secret treasure, he and his family would be able to rebuild what they had lost.

His late brother sired five children. He looked up as the youngest, eight-year-old twins, approached. Julian lowered a box of blackened silverware to the ground, and Jacqueline placed a bent serving tray and three blackened dice on top of it.

"What did you find, Uncle Bernard?"

"Can we see?"

Bernard smiled and rubbed the cool marble. "Our past. And our future. Get the others. We're going on a journey."

IF YOU GIVE A PIRATE A TREASURE
CHAPTER 1

The first letter from Anne Bonny to her father William Cormac:

3 March 1718
Dear Father,

I bid you farewell. I know you disapprove of my choice for a husband. True, he is but a simple sailor. However, I refuse to marry any of those milksops or fortune hunters who continue to darken our door. I love James Bonny and he has sworn his life to me. I ask nothing more from you than your prayers for my health and well-being.

Your daughter,
Anne

July 1811
Harbour Town, South Carolina

Captain Conal O'Brien leaned forward and felt for the linen cloth draped over the foot end of the tub. After wiping his face, he braced his hands on the rim and started to push himself to his feet. He mustn't dawdle if he was going to make it to his sister's wedding on time. His cousin Brendan would learn that he could also dress for an occasion in polished boots and finery. They'd carried on this good-natured rivalry since they were boys.

Conal raised his head, and his nose nearly clipped a pistol barrel. The faint acrid odor of gun powder assailed his nostrils. Focused on the cold, grey metal, he was careful to avoid any sudden movement as he eased himself back into the water. He raised his gaze to peruse the person holding the weapon, a brigand wearing a wide-brimmed hat pulled low. Beneath the hat, a brightly colored scarf covered his hair. Behind the gun bearer stood a second figure, armed as well.

"You have my attention," Conal said evenly. Naked and unarmed. What other choice was there other than negotiation? Although talking his way out of a situation like this wasn't his strength. He was better at negotiating with his fists.

The one holding the pistol stood between him and the lantern, but from what he could ascertain, the intruder was tall, but slight in build. All that prevented Conal from going on the offensive were their weapons.

The closer man must have been thinking along a similar line of thought, because his pistol shook slightly. "This ship has been taken," he said. "If you value your life and the lives of the crew that remain, you will yield."

Crew that *remain*?

Conal's stomach twisted. How had he missed the sound of battle aboard? Granted, all but the watch and a handful of men still making repairs had been allowed to go ashore to attend the wedding celebration, but he should have heard a warning shout or a pistol shot even down here in the galley. How many of his men had lost their lives? He ground his teeth, a silent vow of vengeance burning his throat, guilt trapping it there.

"Do you yield?" The intruder tightened his hold on the pistol.

Conal cursed under his breath. "I yield ye black-hearted spawn of a tavern whore. What are your demands?"

"You will take us and this ship to Jamaica," he said. "Immediately."

Conal tilted his head and narrowed his eyes. The voice sounded too... fragile. A woman, perhaps?

STEVIE SWALLOWED and gripped the pistol handle more firmly. Her arm was beginning to tire from holding it for so long, but she didn't dare lower it. The mountain of a man in the tub looked as if he could crush her head like a grape with one hand, and her young cousin's with the other. More often than not, she could look an average man straight in the eye. However, with this one, she doubted her head would reach his nose.

Stevie and her family had spied on the *Seeker* for hours.

"Look," Uncle Bernard had finally pointed. "Most of the crew is heading to shore. There's only a small watch left behind." He rubbed his chin and peered through the thick fog in the direction of the sun, which was up there somewhere in the late afternoon sky. "This fog bank will provide perfect cover. Let's go. The quicker we get this ship to that devil-pirate Gampo, the quicker he'll return the children to us."

The memory of the pirate's men ripping her little brother and sister from her arms and taking them into the belly of a vessel called the *Dragon* had Stevie checking the priming of her pistol.

Thankfully, she hadn't needed to use it. The remaining crew of the *Seeker* had gathered around an upturned crate and played cards, enabling Stevie and the rest of the family to surround them.

The men had surrendered with barely a word.

It had been a foolhardy plan.

Ridiculous.

Dangerous.

Crazy.

Yet absolutely imperative they succeed.

THE MAN in the tub arched his brows, still awaiting her answer, then his eyes narrowed before sliding down to her soft doeskin boots and back up again. She cursed her stupidity. They should have stayed more in the shadows; it might have given them more of an intimidating appearance.

"Stevie," her young cousin whispered from behind her, bringing her attention back in line. What was the question? Oh, yes. Demands.

"You will relinquish your freedom and possessions," she said, barely able to keep the tremor from her voice. Her gaze paused at the gold signet ring on the man's finger. If they were going to become pirates, she might as well start acting like one. She took a deep breath and drew her shoulders back a little. "Beginning with your ring," she said, holding out her hand.

The man's jaw clenched and the knuckles gripping the tub's edge whitened. He was contemplating his chances of overpowering her and taking her pistol; she could see that in the way his gaze shifted back and forth between her and Gabriel. If he'd had a weapon, and if it had been a one-on-one situation instead of one against two (with guns), he likely wouldn't have paused to contemplate it this long. He would have defended himself by attacking them. And he'd have won. Even now, she sensed he was still calculating his odds.

She eased a step back, careful to keep her pistol well within a lethal range. "Please don't try it," she said. "I'd prefer to save my shot." She was far from her cozy little room off the kitchens of her brother's gaming house. Handling a weapon was only slightly more foreign to her than wearing her cousin's britches. Uncle Bernard had given her a brief lesson on managing a pistol, but it still terrified her to hold it.

His eyes widened and his brows raised in surprise. She'd been right in her assumptions, then. She usually was. Her intuition annoyed her brothers no small amount, and they always avoided her when they wished their thoughts to remain hidden. Only one of them could hide from her, but he was a gambler and so it was expected, otherwise he wouldn't be a very good gambler, would he?

The man twisted the ring from his finger and tossed it to her. She caught it and placed it on the only finger it would fit—her thumb.

Keeping her focus on their hostage, she moved behind him to the stack of clothes on the galley table and removed the dagger and pistol next to them. She'd keep a close watch; he looked like the type of man who'd rather fight against the odds than give himself over. They needed to get him up on deck with the rest of her family before she fainted from the trauma of this whole episode. She came down to the galley to see what stores they had. Finding a man taking a bath was *not* what she'd expected to discover.

"Get dressed," she said, with as much authority as she could muster.

With the oily movement of a cat, he stood, then reached for a linen rag. Stevie felt her eyes widen. She was wrong. *Very wrong.* The top of her head would barely reach his chin, let alone his nose. Wide, thick shoulders rippled as he moved, and took up most of the space in the galley. A long scar trailed across his ribcage. A fighting man. A very strong, very muscular, very handsome, very *naked,* fighting man.

She should shut her eyes, avert her gaze, something…but that would be foolish right now. She'd never seen a naked man as perfectly proportioned as this one. To be honest, she'd only seen one other naked man (other than her terribly immodest brothers while growing up). Her cousin Gabriel's mortified expression from the doorway prompted her to roll her eyes and give him a pointed look he interpreted perfectly. She'd changed his diapers when she was eight. Besides, she was no dainty maiden.

She'd lost her virginity after falling foolishly in love with a gambler who'd promised her a life of love and luxury, then left her the next day. After losing everything he had as well as several hundred dollars in credits to the house, he disappeared and never returned.

He'd crushed her heart. Ruined it. Ruined her.

Worse were the looks of thunderous anger and then pity from her brothers and male cousins. Especially her brother Tristan, who'd tried to warn her, but she'd defended the snake, and refused to listen. It was a painful lesson to learn. Men told a woman anything to sway her attentions to the bedroom, even profess their love and ask for her hand in marriage and persuade her to give him the most precious gift she had.

Their captive turned toward her and reached for his clothes. Her tongue stuck to the roof of her mouth and she could barely swallow. He had a chiseled chest with a faint layer of fine, light brown hair that darkened to a burnished auburn as it trailed past his navel.

Oh, my.

"Satisfied, little rabbit?" he asked. A cocky brow quirked up toward his damp hairline.

So he'd already guessed she was a woman in men's clothing. She assumed he was talking about her perusal, which she wasn't about to address. No need to give him a burst of confidence right now. Besides, her mouth was still dry. Instead, she licked her lips then asked a question. "Little rabbit?" She looked nothing at all like a rabbit. Her ears, along with her hair, were covered.

"You look as if you're ready to jump out of your skin. Perhaps you're afraid of me?" He leaned toward her.

Yes.

"No." She barely managed a response. Her attempt at laughter was pathetic at best.

"Well... little rabbit," his voice was lower than a growl, "you *should* be."

Her heart jerked in a panicked beat and she stepped back.

He dressed. A pair of shiny cordovan boots stood next to the tub, and he pulled them on while muttering obscenities about someone named Brendan. That task complete, he stood up straight, crossed his thick arms over his very impressive chest and glowered at her. His eyes were a grey-green with a golden band around the pupil, reminding her of a tiger she'd once seen in a traveling show. She wanted to swallow, but was paralyzed. Was this how prey felt just before it became the tiger's dinner?

He'd already determined she was female. Now, he was studying her, calculating the odds on a successful confrontation. If he charged her right now, she'd probably squeal and tumble into a terrified heap on the floor, but he needed to believe she'd shoot him. She pulled back the hammer of her pistol until it clicked to help him with his decision-making process, and hopefully to fortify hers. Still, her heart pulsed and throbbed in uneven beats. Running the kitchens in her family's boarding and gaming house was a far cry from being a brigand. Pirating was not on her short list of talents. In fact, she was rather pleased she'd pulled back the hammer without accidentally discharging the gun.

Stevie called over her shoulder to her cousin, inwardly cursing at the way her voice trembled. "Gabriel, if he makes a move toward either of us, shoot him." His hammer clicked behind her.

Good.

Pointing toward the door with the pistol, she gestured for her prisoner to go topside.

Almost soundlessly, he moved in long, sinuous strides through the passageway and up the ladder. He smelled of soap, new leather boots, and a musky scent she knew was all him. The vision of that tiger from long ago crept into her thoughts again as she eyed his movements.

Her thoughts jumped to her family up on the main deck, probably thinking she was taking inventory of the pantry. No one expected she'd find anyone down here, which was a stupid assumption, apparently.

Quite honestly, it was a miracle they'd successfully taken the brigantine.

And this was supposed to be the easy part.

READ BOOK 4: If You Give a Pirate a Treasure today!

AMAZON READERS

For Chloe's new release updates on Amazon, go to the link below, then hit **"Follow"**
http://author.to/ChloeFlowers

DEAR READER

Thank you for reading! Please consider leaving a review, your opinion means a lot to me, and I'd appreciate any feedback you'd like to share.

To sign up for new release alerts: http://chloeflowers.com/contact/

You'll receive book recommendations, recipes the characters in my books cook up, as well as a fun contest or giveaway. You'll also hear about my bee hives! In exchange, I'll send you a free ebook download to read or give to a friend.

Fondly,

Chloe

P.S. Are you an organ donor? I am.

For more information, go to: https://www.organdonor.gov/register.html

You can reach Chloe via snail mail (and if you'd like your print book signed, send it here, along with your return address). She does her best to personally reply to every letter.

❧

Flowers & Fullerton Publishing
303 North Court St.
Box 37
Medina, Ohio 44258

❧

Find Chloe on:
BookBub http://www.bookbub.com/authors/chloe-flowers
Goodreads
http://www.goodreads.com/author/show/15202298.Chloe_Flowers
On Twitter: @flowers_chloe
On Facebook: http://www.facebook.com/chloe.flowersauthor
Website: http://chloeflowers.com
Publisher: www.FlowersandFullerton.com

ABOUT CHLOE

CHLOE SUPPORTS THE NATIONAL BREAST CANCER FOUNDATION.

๛

Chloe Flowers is an award-winning author and the recipient of the University of Akron, Wayne College *2018 Writer of the Year* Award. She writes small town contemporary women's fiction, and historical women's action and adventure romance novels about scoundrels, pirates, and spunky, independent heroines.

Chloe keeps bees and identifies her hives by the different flowers she paints on them. Her pets have always been named after her favorite characters or action heroes: Indiana, Luke, Gimli, Thelma, Rocket, Forrest, Severus, Mushu, Mérida, Gibbs, Jack, and Dead Pool (he's a goldfish).

Chloe's biggest fault is the apparent inability to say "no" whether it's in response to a call for aid or a double-dog-dare to hike home through 30 acres of a snow-covered forest at midnight... during a full moon. It was early morning during said adventure when she came upon a group of sheriff's deputies searching for a lost girl. So, of course she offered to help (turns out, they were searching for her).

She is a member of the Romance Writers of America, Northeast Ohio Romance Writers and RWA Contemporary Romance Writers, The Beau Monde Romance Writers group, where she served as secretary 2017-2019.

She has given workshops and presentations on creating a

critique group, how to provide effective critiques, story structure, marketing and self-publishing lessons to writers' groups, library patrons and school children.

In 2014, she started her own small publishing company, Flowers & Fullerton. Currently, she's the publisher of record for authors Sheridan Jeane, Heather Knight, H.O. Knight as well as herself.

Chloe has a weakness for good red wine, Calvin & Hobbes comics, pie, dark chocolate and brown-eyed guys with beards, which is probably why she digs pirates, men in uniform and treasure hunters and writes about action and adventure and of course romance, which is the greatest adventure of all.

facebook.com/chloe.flowersauthor

twitter.com/flowers_chloe

instagram.com/chloeflowerswrites

bookbub.com/authors/chloe-flowers

pinterest.com/chloeflowers

FRIED PIES

A SOUTHERN RECIPE

I love fried pies!

Fried pies can be filled with anything, meat and cheese, seafood, rice and vegetables or fruit filling. You can use pre-made pie dough or use the recipe below. I also included a yummy filling, which you can spice up or down to your taste, or fill them with leftovers: pot roast, stew, jambalaya, turkey dinner, shrimp gumbo, taco meat and cheese... the possibilities are endless!

Make the filling first:

  1 1/2 pounds of Ground Meat (pork, beef, turkey or a
  mixture)
  1/2 cup Celery, chopped
  1/2 cup Red Pepper, chopped
  1 Onion, chopped (more finely than celery and peppers)
  3 cloves or 1 1/2 Tablespoons of Minced Garlic
  1/2 cup of Cooked Rice (optional)
  1/4 tsp. Cayenne pepper
  1 tsp. Paprika
  1 tsp. Salt

1/2 tsp. Ground Pepper
1/2 tsp. Oregano
1/2 tsp. Thyme
3 Green Onions, chopped
1 cup Water
1 1/2 Tablespoons Flour

Coat a large skillet with about a teaspoon of olive or vegetable oil, then brown the ground meat (to make this a veggie pie, replace meat with 1 cup of cooked rice and one can of black beans-drained).

Add vegetables and spices: onions, peppers, celery, rice, cayenne pepper, paprika, salt, pepper, oregano, thyme. Simmer until vegetables are soft and wilted, (about 10 minutes) then add garlic and cook for a couple minutes more. Add green onions and remove from heat. Mix well and let it cool a bit while you prepare the pastry dough.

PASTRY:

This is the best recipe EVER for home made pie crusts. It's the same pastry dough my husband's grandfather taught my mother-in-law how to make when she was a newlywed. It's an old, tried-and-true family recipe.

Mix the below ingredients well, until it resembles coarse crumbs:

3 Cups Sifted Flour
1 Tablespoon Sugar
1 tsp. Salt
3/4 tsp. Baking Powder
1 1/4 Cup Solid Shortening (such as Crisco, butter, margarine sticks).

Next, combine 1 beaten egg with:

5 Tablespoons of cold water

1 Tablespoon vinegar

Mix the egg mixture into the flour mixture until you are able to form a dough. Separate it into 2 pieces and then flatten them between sheets of wax paper or plastic wrap and put into the refrigerator for 5-10 minutes.

Take the 2 flat dough balls and separate each into 6 pieces, to form 12 total dough balls. Roll each one out to about 5 inches in diameter or 1/4 inch thick. Brush the edges with an egg wash (an egg white mixed well with a teaspoon of water). Put a spoonful (about 1/4 cup or so) of the meat mixture on one half, fold the other half over it, and press the edges together. You can roll the edges to seal them or crimp them with a fork.

To fry the pies: Heat vegetable oil, peanut oil or Crisco in a pan. They will fry better if they have about 1/2 inch of hot oil to cook in. Brown on both sides, remove with a slotted spoon and drain on paper towels until cool enough to eat. (5 minutes).

To bake the pies: Preheat oven to 400 degrees (F), brush the tops of all the pies with the egg wash and arrange on a cookie sheet with about 1/2 inch of space between them (at least). Bake for 15 minutes or until golden brown.

P.S. This pie crust recipe also makes 3 regular sized pie crusts.

Find the recipes for other dishes in the books on Chloe's website: www.chloeflowers.com